Seasons

Gay Sizemore Sauer

iUniverse, Inc.
New York Bloomington

SEASONS

iUniverse books may be ordered through booksellers or by contacting:

iUniverse
1663 Liberty Drive
Bloomington, IN 47403
www.iuniverse.com
1-800-Authors (1-800-288-4677)

ISBN: 978-1-4401-6525-2 (sc)
ISBN: 978-1-4401-6523-8 (dj)
ISBN: 978-1-4401-6524-5 (ebk)

Printed in the United States of America

iUniverse rev. date: 10/26/2009

Seasons

These pages are dedicated to the memory of my
grandmothers,
Ollie Cleo Sizemore
and
Ollie Pearl Littlefield,
whose wisdom and charm
sustained and inspired

Author's note

The central character in the stories, the old woman in the wheelchair, is a composite figure drawn from many older people I have been privileged to know. Her life's circumstances change from story to story, so there is no fixed identity. She symbolizes a loving figure who has grown old but has not lost her love for life or her fellow man—nor has she lost that wonderful memory that she uses to make sense out of her present circumstances.

This collection of stories is an outgrowth of a ministry carried out by the United Methodist Women's Unit of Columbia United Methodist Church in West Columbia, Texas. We visited the Country Village Assisted Living Community in Angleton, Texas, once a month. I would write a story for the residents, and several of us baked cookies to be passed out to them after story time. The popularity of the stories encouraged me to compile them for publication.

For many years I have been a careful observer of that generation of loved ones and friends in nursing homes around the country. It saddens me to see those who seem lost to the present, vegetating silently. My prayer is that they are simply lost in the pleasant world of their memories, something like the old woman in the wheelchair is inclined to do. It is always a joy to find old people who are mentally alert and able to continue to be interested in the world around them. There are many of them, and they need daily stimulation.

My own sense is that much more could be done for our older population, but the burden cannot be placed on the staffs of nursing homes. The families and friends of these old people must continue to love and care for them on a frequent and regular basis. Volunteer groups such as United Methodist Women are helpful, but it is the tender touch of a loved one or a hug from a friend of many years that makes the light truly shine in the eyes of these older people.

One character in the stories is drawn from real life, my old friend Nadine Scruggs. I was her friend for many years before she was placed in assisted living, and my mother and I were faithful in our visits and attention to her. She was part of UMW's story circle until her death at the age of 102. She was mentally alert to the very end, and was a strong inspiration for me to be of service to Country Village.

Another figure named in one of the stories is my mother-in-law, Tillie Sauer, who resides at Bowdle Nursing Home in South Dakota. She will be 102 August 17, 2009. Even when she seems completely lost to the present, her sweet and loving nature is apparent.

Want to perform a service? Visit a nursing home and adopt one of these old people to lavish your love and interest upon. The rewards are soul-satisfying.

January

The New Year and the raw landscape
stretch forth, a blank canvas
awaiting the touch of
human endeavor
and the
creative blessing
of God.

About Storms and Courage

Ten or twelve residents in the nursing home were gathered around the television in the large reception area. There were other televisions in small living rooms throughout the home, and the residents also had televisions in their bedrooms, but they liked this one. It was not only large, but it was placed in a great center of activity—the nurses' station was not far away, and one door opened to the outside, from which visitors regularly emerged. They liked the large screen, but they liked even better the sounds of activity, both within their world and from the world without.

One elderly resident especially liked to be here. This old woman in the wheelchair enjoyed the presence of the others around her, because it reminded her of the large family she had grown up in. She liked the noise and clatter of activity, because large families always made a variety of sounds, and the noise made her feel at home. She reluctantly admitted that she also enjoyed the television programs. Before coming here, she rarely watched television, but now some of the programs had become part of her life. She followed the game shows and soap operas with great interest.

Many times the stories on television made her think of people she had known in her more active life. Those people had mostly turned out all right in the end, and she sensed the same would be true for the soap opera characters. As she watched the screen, she was startled when the program was interrupted to announce a storm alert. Very dangerous weather was approaching the area, and everyone was ordered to take cover and stay indoors. It was a very dangerous electrical storm, the announcer warned.

The old woman had to smile. It was unlikely many of them would be going outdoors, in this or any other kind of weather. Theirs had become a mostly indoor existence. They sat around in the nursing home every day in a routine of comfort and security. Most of them were in wheelchairs, as she was, and some of them, like herself, had outlived most of their friends and many of their relatives.

She thought how misleading the appearance of their lives must be to those who looked on. She knew onlookers would be surprised if they could follow the thoughts she regularly entertained. What an active mind she had! She knew many of the others around her also liked to be entertained by their thoughts. Most of them could sit quietly, reminiscing about the years when their lives intertwined more actively with the lives of those they had loved. They could be drawn from their reminiscing, but it took effort. Sadly, the old woman knew that even their loved ones often didn't have the time or patience to make that effort.

Another announcement came on the television, warning of terrible weather approaching. Then the television went off, as did the lights in the room. A few cries of dismay broke the silence, but it was mostly irritation that the program was gone, rather than fear of what might come next.

She remembered many occasions in her life when bad weather interrupted the life of the family. In her youth, the winter months, especially January, were bad weather times. When she was just a little girl, six or seven at the most, she could not attend school for an entire month one January because the snow had piled up, and no wagon or car could get through. Her family lived in the country, several miles from town. It was a bad storm, and there was no electricity in the house.

She remembered candles being placed around the farmhouse in the evening. The chores must be done, whatever the weather, but to her surprise, school lessons must be done, too! She recalled the candlelit scenes around the kitchen table, after dishes were washed and put away. Her parents sat down with their children, and they went over the lessons with their little girls. Although at the time she may have preferred taking the candle and her book to a corner near the fireplace to read, in later years, she thought of the family gathered around the table as a perfect family remembrance.

Patiently, her father explained the arithmetic lessons to his little girls. The mother, in turn, would read the little paragraphs they had written and correct their errors. Then she would make them rewrite the paragraphs. "Until we got it right!" the old woman always said when telling the story to later generations. She knew the family circle she described to them must have seemed idyllic, but she also knew that every word she used to describe it was true.

Later she learned of the hard days her father had spent helping other farmers clear a path to town so that they and their families would not be isolated from the community they depended on in emergencies. She did not keep count of the days at the time, but in later years, she'd learned the family had been stranded for nearly two weeks before the roads and weather cleared.

The days had not been wasted; far from it. The family had drawn even closer together because of the storm. They had plenty of food. The produce from her mother's garden, all carefully harvested and canned for the winter, kept them well fed. Meat from her father's smokehouse had been brought into the kitchen when the first signs of the storm occurred. It seemed like her parents were the patriarchs in the Old Testament. She thought of Joseph in Egypt, dealing with the seven lean years.

That reminded her of the family Bible reading that went on in that farmhouse. When lessons were done, the family gathered around the hearth and listened as her father read the scriptures. He read passages from both the Old and New Testaments before prayers were said and the girls were sent to their bedroom.

The old woman thought about the presence of storms in the lives of people. They were dangerous things, storms, and she knew a fair number of stories about people who lost their lives because they did not respect the power of storms. She remembered an incident when she was first married. A bad electrical storm—again, in January—had brought the power lines down. Some men in the neighborhood thought the power company was too slow in making its repair, so they decided to repair the lines themselves. Their decision was both foolish and fatal. One of them was electrocuted while grappling with a loose wire. Even as she grieved with her neighbors over the loss of this man, she couldn't help but compare his effort with that of her father so many years ago. Both were trying to provide a sense of community and comfort to their families. Both went out because a storm had threatened their family's safety. Both had exemplified great love and courage. One acted with great patience, and the other was heedless in the face of danger.

As a young woman comparing the efforts of these two men of different generations, she recalled a verse her father often read from the Bible: "I will wait upon the Lord." Her father had shown patience. The path to town was not cleared in a day; it had taken many days. The clearing had not taken place while the storm was raging, but after it had passed.

As the winds whirled around the nursing home, the old woman quietly prayed for the safety of those who were out in the storm. She prayed they would have patience to "wait upon the Lord" and be grateful for the shelter He provided. She thanked the Lord for the nursing home and for the loving care she received there. It was not unlike that farmhouse scene of so many, many years ago.

As she looked about her, she imagined that the fireplace of her childhood would now be the television screen, and the kitchen table full of activity would be the nurse's station. The fireplace and kitchen table represented the love and security she had felt in her childhood home, and she understood why the television, with its colorful screen, and the busy nurse's station would give her a sense of security in her old age.

She smiled sweetly in the fading light at the other residents around her. They were associated in her mind with her sisters, each completely comfortable in the safety of this place. She knew her rambling associations made little sense to anyone else, but it was enough that it made sense to her. Many things that made perfect sense to her would meet with startled expressions if she tried to explain them to others, so she had learned to keep many of her thoughts to herself.

It was nearing her naptime, and she indicated to one of the nurses that she wanted to be taken to her room.

When she was comfortable in her bed, she thought again about the storms of life. She knew it took courage and patience for anyone to deal with them. Even if she was confined to a wheelchair, she knew she had courage. Patience was something else, however, and when she said her prayers, she would include a reference to this shortcoming, even as she gave thanks for the safety and security she enjoyed in the midst of the storm.

Fluency

Ideas are teeming in my mind,
Clamoring to get out.
They range in thoughts of every kind,
And circle all about.

They vie with one another
Each time I try to speak;
Expression thus is smothered
In a verbalized retreat.

Order! Get some order!
And go one at a time.
Without some decent order,
This effort will not rhyme!

Sort yourselves out, please,
Establish rank and file.
Establish continuity,
Banish fluff and guile.

On your mark, Idea One:
You can now parade.
Get set—don't let
Your impact fade.

Now go—march on,
Unfettered, free.
Express yourself in
Clean, clear strides,

And explain
Some part of me.

Puzzles

The old woman had moved her wheelchair to the table where a jigsaw puzzle had been set out for the residents. The five-hundred-piece puzzle was that of a forest scene with small animals in the foreground. The puzzle she had worked last week was a rural scene with farm buildings in the background, and the foreground was dominated by a herd of dairy cows. She much preferred cows to squirrels, at least in a puzzle, but she chose not to complain but to be thankful that puzzles were provided.

Some years ago she had read that keeping the mind active with puzzles was a recommended way to keep the brain healthy. Consequently, she had worked thousands of crossword puzzles and other word games, as well as jigsaw puzzles. In her childhood, jigsaw puzzles had been a family activity her parents had encouraged, because it kept the children quiet and near at hand.

Quiet? Their fitting the pieces together may have been quiet at the outset when sorting them into kindred piles, but as the race to complete the puzzle accelerated, noise erupted from all corners of the table. She remembered that one of her sisters had the selfish habit of keeping three or four pieces in a pocket away from the scrutiny of the others. Thus she would be master of the puzzle, placing the very last pieces in place, not unlike the person who always has to have the last word on any subject. It had all been fun, however, and was much more satisfying than working on the puzzle alone, as she was doing now.

First she sorted all the border pieces. Her parents had taught her that the border had to be in place first. As she began to assemble the border, she thought about its function, and she came to the conclusion that, like most things, borders had good and bad points. Borders were definitions and were therefore inclusive. The reverse had to be true as well, for they excluded. Still, as Robert Frost pointed out in his poem "Mending Wall," so many years ago, "Good Fences make good neighbors."

She tried to remember how the poem began, because it seemed to contradict the last line. Ah yes. "Something there is that doesn't love a wall."

Borders, walls, fences; these seem to be manmade constructions that declared ownership. For her part, having been reared on a farm, she saw the logic in good fences, and indeed, they did make good neighbors. They kept feisty livestock from destroying a neighbor's garden. She remembered more than one occasion when her mother's garden was all but ripped up by the roots by the neighbor's bull, who never got the knack of recognizing property lines.

Had civilization managed to get out of hand with its notions of ownership? She also recalled one of William Wordsworth's poems, "The World Is Too Much With Us." As a student, she was always saddened when she read the line, "Little we see in nature that is ours." For her part, nature was the province of those who loved it, and she ran at will over the acres of her father's farm, loving the progress of the seasons. She recognized the limits of her exploration, however, and realized that somewhere in her youth, her parents had taught her to respect the property borders of the area.

On at least one occasion she forgot. She and her brother were down by the creek, picking wild plums. The tree on the other side of the fence was laden with the prettiest ripe plums they had yet seen. They got under the barbed wire fence on their bellies and walked to the tree. Picking the plums was quickly accomplished, for they had grown in thick clumps. Their pails were almost full when they saw a second tree bursting with ripe plums, even further from the fence.

She could still remember the scolding they received when they returned to the farmhouse. The neighbor, on whose property the two plum trees grew, had taken note of their trespassing and was undisturbed until he saw his two plum trees being delivered of their harvest, so he complained to their father. His wife had been keeping track of those two trees, he said, for they were to supply fruit she would use for jelly making.

She recalled the humiliation she and her brother felt when their father made them take their buckets of plums to the neighbors and apologize. The neighbor's wife protested, "Oh, you haven't picked so many. For goodness sake, there's enough for everyone. I'll still have plenty for my jelly making." She made the children return home with their buckets of plums.

Walls, fences, borders; they can be good things if they define property between people who respect one another.

When there is no respect, hostilities can develop. She had been a pretty good history student in her youth, and she knew that more than one war had developed over border disputes. These wars stretched back in time as far as there were people to write the history books. Sadly, they still kept the world on edge. Thankfully, there were some good neighbors among the nations, like the neighbor's wife, who knew there were enough plums for everyone.

"There!" the old woman said aloud. She had put the last border piece in place. At about this time, she heard the approach of another resident.

"I was working that puzzle," the person approaching said in a petulant voice. "I had nearly all the border finished before I left to take my nap."

"Isn't there puzzle enough for both of us?" the old woman said pleasantly, remembering the plums.

The unpleasant person mumbled something that the old woman in the wheelchair took to be proprietary control of the puzzle. Fence-building!

The old woman in the wheelchair backed from the table and said she had a crossword puzzle she needed to finish.

"What's a four-letter word that means selfish?" the old woman said in spite of herself, but not really loud enough for the other person to hear.

The other person, bent over the puzzle, did not bother to look up, even if she could guess the answer: *rude.*

What had Frost called such an unfriendly neighbor? A Neanderthal!

Chuckling in good humor, the old woman headed toward the home's library, where she could locate the crossword puzzle from the newspaper.

"That is, if someone else hasn't gotten to it first!"

February

The forced retreat indoors
provides reflection,
for the counting
of blessings,
not the least of which
is the comfort
of a fireside surrounded
by the presence of loving friends.

Heart-shaped

The old woman sat in front of the large picture window, looking out upon the nursing home's flower garden. No flowers were there, for it was the middle of February. Several more weeks were required for the garden to burst into bloom. She peered closely to see if there were traces of green among the frosty branches of the shrubbery. There were none yet, but she knew life was in those branches. What they needed was the sun's warmth to reveal their true beauty.

The woman was filled with a quiet satisfaction as she looked out at the cold, barren garden. How warm and comfortable she was inside the building, completely at ease. It was Valentine's Day, and yesterday her granddaughter had visited with a vase of red roses and a beautiful card. She had always enjoyed the love of her family and even admitted that she was spoiled.

"I love you, Grandmother, and wanted you to have these flowers in your room when you opened your eyes on Valentine's Day," her granddaughter had told her.

Indeed, the roses had been the first thing to capture her attention this morning. What a powerful thing love is, she reflected. She thought of it as the sunshine in life. It had always sustained her, never more so than now, in her old age. When she could do so little for herself, the love of others made these years not only tolerable, but also blessed.

The old woman thought about Valentine's Day and what it had meant to her throughout her life. Ah, she remembered that cold day in February when she was about eight or nine years old. Her mother had gathered the little sisters around the kitchen table and provided them with red paper, crayons, and envelopes. They were instructed to make valentines for all the boys and girls in their class.

"No!" she had protested. "Valentines are just for people you like. I don't like everyone in my class."

She especially had in mind two classmates she carefully avoided. Although it would be years before she understood the meaning of *haughty,* she clearly exhibited haughtiness at an early age. She did not like this boy or girl, because she considered them unworthy of her notice. They seemed to wear the same clothes, day in and day out. The boy went weeks and weeks before he got a haircut, and the girl's long, red hair was as wild and untamed as her behavior.

"No," the young girl repeated to her mother. "I do not want to give a Valentine to *everyone.*"

In the end, of course, her mother had prevailed, and she was made to do the right thing.

Why was it so hard to do the right thing, the old woman wondered as she recalled her childish rebellion. What were two more Valentines, when all the materials for making them were on the table right in front of her? Doing the right thing was more than crayon and paper, of course. It was a softening of the heart—a willingness to overlook the small things that divide people.

When the Valentines were distributed in class the next day, she was surprised at the reaction of the boy and girl she had wanted to ignore. The boy came up to her, shyly looked into her eyes, and said, "Thank you. I made you one, too."

He handed her a hastily contrived Valentine made of tablet paper. She had seen him making it while the Valentines were being distributed. It was inscribed, "To my friend." She was strangely touched as she looked into the boy's steady blue eyes.

The red-haired girl had made no last-minute Valentine, but she too came up to the girl and said something pleasant about friendship, adding, "I am so glad you are my friend."

The old woman nestled into the comfort of her wheelchair and tried to think if anything memorable happened that year other than the exchange of Valentines. No single event came to mind, but the girl with the flaming red hair eventually mastered her behavior. Somewhere along the passage of elementary to high school, she managed to obtain some decent clothes for herself. Most remarkable of all, by the time she reached high school, she had become a scholar. Her thirst for learning was impressive.

The boy's development was even more impressive. He had secured small part-time jobs in the community and developed a sterling reputation for hard work and integrity. The community's businessmen followed his progress with keen interest.

Although she grew to admire both of them, the young girl was never particularly close to either through the remainder of their school days. She was pleased, however, when the red-haired girl, graduating valedictorian in their class, went to college on scholarships that would prepare her to be a teacher. The boy, third in the class, earned acceptance at a medical school, thanks to all the businessmen, including the town doctor, who underwrote his expenses there. Even now, the old woman, looking back on the unlikely careers of these two classmates, marveled at their success.

Some years later, when she was married and had several children of her own, she was astonished to meet the red-haired classmate again at the opening of school. Her old classmate would be the teacher of her oldest girl. The woman had to admit that, at the conclusion of that school year, her daughter had never had such a fine teacher.

Her heart had been deeply touched when, during the first week in February, her daughter's teacher sent home a letter to parents, instructing them to see that their children made Valentines for all their classmates. Perhaps no parent of a child in that class knew better that she the inspiration for that letter.

The woman's other three children eventually had the red-haired teacher, and they loved her every bit as much as the oldest child had. Years after their education was completed, and this included college, her children agreed that this teacher was their favorite. She had taught them the most, and they believed with all their hearts that she loved them.

The old woman remembered that, after retiring, the teacher and her husband had moved to England. She had lost track of her after that, but often thought of her, always with love, and especially on Valentine's Day.

The other classmate, the small boy whose eyes had looked so earnestly into hers that Valentine's Day so long ago, had become a very good doctor, serving the townspeople for generations. Yes, he had returned to the town that had supported him when he had no other means of help. He demonstrated through his medical practice the power of love as the best medicine.

When her husband broke his leg stumbling over a chair in the middle of the night, a Sunday night at that, her old classmate set it and put it in a cast. The leg healed perfectly, in no small part due to the doctor's knowledge and skill. The doctor was inclined to make house calls, long after other doctors had abandoned the practice. His willingness to take care of those who could not pay was well known. When asked why he did so much for others, he turned those steady, gazing eyes on the one asking the question and replied, "Because so much was done for me."

On Valentine's Day the old woman would think about these two classmates in terms of their remarkable life achievements. On other days, in her reflections, they were simply her friends, her equals.

"Oh my," she said. "Equals? I'd say *superiors*, surely."

The Valentines she unwillingly made and gave to them were the first small steps she took toward recognizing the genuine worth of a person. Never again did she allow appearances to mislead her in her estimation of a person's character. She allowed that those two had far more to teach her about the human spirit than she had to show them the refinements of society.

She had to smile—here they had eclipsed her, too! Life was funny, and how good that she could still laugh at the absurd little girl she had been.

In the middle of her laugh, she heard the approach of another wheelchair. She turned to see her old classmate and friend, the doctor, wheel up to her. His old, arthritic hand was stretched toward her, and in it was a Valentine.

"For you," he said. "My son and daughter brought me a large packet of them earlier in the week and said I must give one to all my friends here. This one is especially pretty, and I saved it for you."

The old woman clasped the Valentine to her heart, and with misty eyes, looked up at him. Remarkable! He still had that steady, serious gaze she remembered from grade-school days.

What if the flowers in the garden outside never bloomed? The power of love and friendship in a Valentine was sufficient to warm the heart at any age.

"I have a bouquet of lovely roses," the old woman said to her friend. "I want to share them with you. It will only take me a minute or two to locate a proper vase."

On the Occasion of a Friend's Visit

"What is a friend?" you asked.
I said I'd think about it and let you know.

Now that I've considered all the trite
And tiresome word offerings placed on
The altar of friendship,

I've decided that a friend is one who in
Your mind produces images that make you happy:

A song, a favorite refrain,
More loved for being heard again;

A burst of flowers on a favorite hill,
Pots of geraniums on the window sill.

The unexpected sun on a February day,
The promise of summer coming, felt in May.

My list could ramble *ad infinitum*
(that's what lists are designed to do),
So to answer your question succinctly,
More distinctly,

A friend is someone like you.

What Am I Missing?

The old woman in the wheelchair looked through the small drawer in her bedside table. "I know I placed it somewhere," she muttered in puzzlement.

She was looking for her watch, a possession precious because her husband had given it to her many years ago. Anything he had given her was a treasured precious reminder of the great love they had shared. She looked everywhere in the room where she might have put it. An uncomfortable suspicion began to gnaw at her: did someone take it? Who would do such a thing?

"I mustn't start harboring thoughts like that," she sensibly told herself. "There is no reason to believe anyone would have taken it. For one thing, it is valuable only to myself, and for another, it never kept good time anyway. Anyone wanting to steal a watch would have better choices

Comforted by her own assurances, she moved away from the bedside table and turned to face the television. Seeking diversion, she said, "I'll just watch a program or two before going to the dining room."

Before reaching for her remote control, which she kept beside her on the wheelchair, she picked up the Bible she kept on the table at the foot of her bed. She read it daily, skipping around through both testaments. She especially loved reading psalms, but this morning, her Bible seemed to open itself to the fifth chapter of Deuteronomy. She began to read the list of commandments that God, through Moses, had given the children of Israel.

There it was: "Thou shalt not steal." She was reminded again of her missing watch, along with the uncomfortable feeling that someone could have taken it.

What makes people take things that do not belong to them? She believed that everyone at some time or another had taken something. Apparently it was a human failing, common enough for the Ten Commandments to include it. She remembered her sainted mother trying to teach her little girls about the importance of respecting the property of others. She often told them, "For goodness sake, never take something that does not belong to you."

Her mother used a personal illustration to make her point. As a little girl, she herself had once taken something. She had visited a little friend in the neighborhood and greatly admired a colored-glass ink bottle that rested on a windowsill. Its perch allowed the bottle to reflect the sun, and the beauty of this proved irresistible to her. On her way out, she put the bottle in her coat pocket. Of course her own mother saw it immediately when she returned home and asked why she had taken it. "Because it was so pretty in the light," the small girl mumbled, hanging her head in shame.

"You are to march right back this moment to your friend's house and return the bottle and apologize for what you have done." The little girl protested, wanting her mother to return it, but her protests fell on deaf ears. She had taken it; she must return it.

The walk back to her friend's house was painful, but handing over the ink bottle to her friend was much worse. Increasing her humiliation, she saw her friend's mother standing in the background, watching the strange transaction of confession and restitution. Apparently this childhood experience had affected her mother deeply, for she used the illustration many times as she strove to bring up her little girls to be honest and respectful of the property of others.

The old woman well remembered the day a younger sister took a miniature pecan pie from the local grocery store without paying for it. She could still picture her mother grabbing that sister by the ear and marching her back to the store, making her return the pie with apologies.

It seemed funny at the time—the pie had only cost a dime. But her mother had told the story of the colored ink bottle too many times to let the infraction go unpunished. To the best of the old woman's knowledge, this little sister never took anything again and grew up to be a model of honesty.

The old woman remembered her own experiences with theft and realized that, in spite of her mother's best intentions, she had not always been entirely honest. Temptation is seductive and subtle.

At the age of ten or eleven, she found a dollar bill on the school bus on the floorboard beneath the seat in front of her. She managed to work the bill with her foot back toward herself, and so far she had not sinned. How many times afterwards had she wished she had announced to those around her that she had found a dollar bill. Instead, she bent over toward her shoe, picked the dollar bill up, and crumpled it in her fist, later depositing it in her coat pocket. That was the point at which she sinned, for she knew very well that dollar belonged to someone else, and she had taken it.

For a few days, she was the owner of a dollar bill, which, though not technically stolen, did not really belong to her. She didn't tell anyone about it, and for the life of her, could never remember what she spent it on. What she did remember with great clarity was something that happened to her the following year.

She had left her coin purse and book bag in the gym locker room after dressing out for volleyball. When she returned to the locker room, her little purse was gone. She cried loudly about the loss, but no one around her even remembered that she had a coin purse. The gym teacher was no help, either. Whoever had taken her purse completely escaped detection. She didn't mind losing the purse, but it held two dollars in it, and it was money entrusted to her by her mother. She had been told to walk to town after school and pay a bill her mother owed. What would she do now?

The consequences of this petty theft affected her in many directions. The most immediate was the question of where she would get the money to replace what was stolen from her.

Stolen. What an ugly word! She remembered that she had worked for neighbors to earn two dollars, and her mother's bill was paid. A consequence of far greater significance was the indelible feeling she had of retribution. She had pocketed a dollar that did not belong to her; now she had been deprived of two dollars. She had to admit there was a twisted turn of justice in her loss.

That was not the end of it. Several years later, on a school band trip to another city, she again was the victim of theft. Her wallet had disappeared, and no amount of searching the bus provided a clue. She was aware of the irony; only this was a loss of much more than a dollar. She had no funds for the entirety of that weekend trip.

The lesson of this second loss made a great impression on her. If the example of her mother's colored-ink-bottle story helped her with honesty during her formative years, the loss of her billfold made her a confirmed believer in the Seventh Commandment, "Thou Shalt Not Steal."

In subsequent years, things might have been stolen from her, but she was entirely trustworthy herself. Thanks to her mother's diligent instruction and her own life's experiences, she realized that there is pain in theft—pain for the one who has lost something, but also the pain of guilt borne by the person who has taken it. It is a pain so easily avoided: don't take what isn't yours, and you spare everyone, yourself included!

It was time she headed to the dining room. Perhaps her tablemates would have some advice for her about the loss of her watch. She reached at her side to find the remote control so it could be put back on her pillow, where she liked to leave it when she left the room.

"What's this?" She picked up the remote control, but felt the cool, familiar touch of metal under it. It was her watch!

"As old as I am, I still must learn lessons about life. Just a moment ago I was obsessed with fear that I had lost something. But it wasn't lost at all. I am grateful I didn't cause a great alarm or point fingers at anyone. That's the very kind of thing a lot of us older folks do."

The old woman knew there must be a lesson in this somewhere. What was she missing? Not a watch; that had been found.

"I need to accept that stuff is just stuff. But I surely am glad I found my watch."

"This heavy thinking has made me hungry. I hope they are serving something delicious for lunch."

The old woman put her watch on her wrist and wheeled her chair toward the dining room.

March

The wind is blowing with all its might
And I just hope that Shelley's right.
Winter, you came and blew right through,
And we have had enough of you.
Spring, you're welcome any time,
Pray tell, are you far behind?

March is for the Strong

The old woman sat near a window, where she could look out at the signs of spring returning to the land. It had been a long winter, and she gave the shrubbery, the trees, and herself a congratulatory salute. "We've made it again," she said as she nodded to the garden beyond the window.

She had always looked upon the month of March as a great seasonal challenge. Someone many generations ago had described March as "in like a lion, out like a lamb." She knew whoever said that must have been someone who thought pretty much the same way she did.

March demanded the best a person had in strength, resourcefulness, and patience. That would be the *lion* in the month, roaring its windy way through the first week or two. Folks who got into the habit of toughing it out ran the danger of ignoring the gentler side of their personalities, the more lamb-like characteristics that described the end of March.

The old woman's thoughts went naturally to her husband, that dear man who had been her life partner for more than sixty years. He was a child of March, for sure, and more often than not, he had been the lion. During their early years especially, it took his lion-hearted courage and strength to keep their family safe and secure. Too often, she admitted, she had taken his magnificent courage for granted, because he had risen to every challenge repeatedly throughout his life. For her part, she rose to the challenge every year of surviving the month of March with her faith and soul intact. March was not her favorite month.

When they had first married, an economic depression was sweeping wildly across the country, and job security was unheard of. Prudent people—and she knew she and her young husband were especially careful with their resources—were very careful to save what they could, because there were no guarantees that a job and income would be there after the next check was cashed.

They had not been inclined to bank their money. Too many terrible stories had circulated about bank failures. They had their own hiding place for the money they had set aside for adversity. It was in an old duffel bag they kept under the bed. She dreamed of the day when the bag was stuffed so full of savings they would be unable to shove it back beneath the bed. Even after several years, the bag's flat outer appearance failed to indicate its hidden assets, and it was still easily moved back and forth from its hiding place.

This financial arrangement might have continued for the rest of their lives together had their house not caught fire during the first week of March after they had been married several years. By then they had two little girls and another child on the way. They had survived the Depression, but some habits do not die easily, and the duffel bag was still their "in-house bank account" to handle their growing family emergencies.

A fire engulfed their house that windy March evening. The fire was started by lightning hitting a tall pine tree outside the front window. It did a lot of damage to the front wall and the roof as it fell, but the fire that followed was especially destructive.

She remembered the terrible crashing sound, and her involuntary scream. Whether it was her scream or the crash, her little girls were startled in the back bedroom where they had been playing. Her husband was outside, securing the livestock and outbuildings. By the time he could get to the house, flames were easily seen through the kitchen window.

Her first thought was to reach the little girls and get them out of the house. Somewhere between the kitchen, where she had been standing at the sink when the lightning struck, and the bedroom, where the girls were screaming, she fainted. She would learn later about the heroics that saved her and the little girls.

Her husband grabbed an ax and broke open the back doorway, screaming the names of his wife and little girls. Miraculously, the little girls had made their way to their mother in the hallway. Using strength he did not know he had, the young husband lifted his wife into his arms and ordered the little girls to grab the legs of his overhauls. "Do not, under any circumstances, let go!" he shouted at them.

As he retraced his steps to the door he had shattered, the man sent up a prayer of thanksgiving for all the lessons of discipline and clear communication he had witnessed his wife give their daughters. The girls understood and obeyed. Within a minute, the family was clear of the house. With great relief, they saw the advance of firefighting equipment and their neighbors rushing toward them. An ambulance following the fire truck was soon put to good use, because she went into premature labor and was taken to the hospital.

The fire was soon extinguished. The house was severely damaged, but repairs would put it right again. The newspapers had a field day with the story, uncertain which headline would attract the most readers: "Father saves his family," or "Mother gives birth after fire nearly destroys home." It was a human-interest story of the first magnitude.

Neighbors had cleared the house of all that could be saved and stored it in the barn. Several weeks later, the woman remembered, she had been surveying what had been salvaged, and with some shock, gazed upon the old duffel bag. There it was among sundry other household goods, unscathed, with all its contents still in place.

She recalled the serious conversation she and her husband later had about the duffel bag and their habit of using it to store money. They agreed that this was one habit that had to change, and a day or two later he placed the money in a saving's account at the local bank.

She had sometimes accused her husband of thinking more about the prospects of prosperity and getting ahead than he did about the comforts she and the girls yearned for. Yet when the chips were down—and literally aflame!— he risked everything in order to save them. She recalled with a shudder some of the burns on his arms and the loss of his hair to the flames. Miraculously, he had managed to save her and both girls without any of them having a single blister.

While the house was being partially rebuilt, she stayed in the hospital with the new baby. The family doctor insisted she stay there until she was completely able to cope with the demands of resettling her house. Toward the end of March, she felt strong enough to go home. It was a very different March now. Flowers and shrubbery were abloom everywhere in the countryside, and the balmy breeze was mild enough for the new baby to face without discomfort.

Gentleness was apparent everywhere she looked. The landscape was soft, and its patterns were contoured with new growth. And her house! It seemed twice the size as before, because a new wing of two bedrooms had been added. How could all this have happened in just a few weeks?

Her neighbors had filled her in on the extraordinary accomplishments of her husband. He had labored night and day, long after the workers had left. His intention was that the house would be set completely to rights by the time his wife and son were ready to come home.

Yes, he had the courage of a lion and the strength of a lion. But when she remembered the soft touch of his big hands as he reached for their new baby, she thought of him as the most endearing lamb in the world. In her estimation, he was a true son of March. How wonderful and necessary were these two aspects of his character.

They lived in that house for many, many years after that, and no further mishaps occurred. The old duffel bag had long since taken up residence in the barn, hanging from a nail. It held various odd bits and pieces that "might come in useful some day." So the duffel bag, she laughed to herself, had certainly held true to its character, yielding its interior for useful storage.

Lions and lambs—what an unlikely combination. Then she remembered what the Bible said about this. She looked at Isaiah 11:6 and read, "The wolf shall dwell with the lamb, and the leopard shall lie down with the kid, and the calf and the lion and the fatling together—and a little child shall lead them."

The old woman recounted the many months of March throughout her life, and she came to the conclusion that the strange mixture of volatility and serenity made it unique. There was danger in the month, as there is danger in the lion, but the strength of the lion was, at the same time, the antidote to danger. She warned herself not to get too complicated pursuing these images. It would interfere with the nap she intended to take. She thought it sufficient that she accept the full personality of March and acknowledged all the good fortune it had blown her way.

The old woman smiled at the buds of new leaves appearing on the tree beyond the window. They had weathered the winter, and now, soft as lamb's wool, they would unfurl and bless the season.

Easter Rock

The heavy heart is burdened
With cares it cannot solve
The soul seems strongly fettered
By weight it can't resolve.
The tears that blind the vision
Course down a saddened face
That tries to find solutions
In a world of waning grace.
To free the heart of sadness
And praise each blessed day
Relive the Easter message: Let
The stone be rolled away.

Sailing Along

"Grand!" called out a dear, familiar voice. It was her great-granddaughter walking through the door, rousing the old woman from her catnap.

She had been lying on her bed, resting, as she often did mid-morning before going to the activity room. Her great-granddaughter's appearance at just this time caused her to suspect that the day would now take a different direction. The old woman was puzzled: Beth took her out to lunch maybe once a month, but that was on the calendar for next week. What brought her here today?

"I'm taking you to lunch!" Beth said as she leaned over to kiss her great-grandmother's cheek. "It's a great surprise, isn't it? I couldn't wait until next week. Something has come up, but if it's okay with you, we can go today. I have already alerted the nursing staff."

As if on cue, a nurse walked in to help Beth get her great-grandmother into her wheelchair. "I'll need my hair brushed," said the old woman.

The nurse brushed the thinning gray hair into place and gave the old woman a hug. "You are lovely enough to show up at anyone's restaurant," she said.

All that remained was to see the old woman safely to Beth's waiting car. Between the nurse and Beth, this was accomplished smoothly. Not for the first time, the old woman gave thanks for the loving care of the nursing home's staff.

"What's the occasion for this surprise, Beth?" The old woman was still befuddled over the unannounced change in plans.

"Oh, Grand, I wanted to tell you over lunch. Can you wait until then?"

Patience had never been among the old woman's virtues, but since she had been in the rest home, it was a trait she worked daily to develop. Surrounded as she was by many whose physical situations were more challenging than her own, patience simply had to be utilized. Otherwise, she knew, chaos would overrule every decent instinct and good intention.

The old woman was glad to admire the scenery as they drove to the edge of town. Their favorite restaurant was located just off the road, in a spot secluded by a grove of trees. It was popular with people in the area, and the old woman and her family had been patrons for years.

Beth had obviously planned this well, for a waiter came from the restaurant to help the old woman with her wheelchair while her great-granddaughter parked the car. Minutes later, Beth rejoined her, and they were ushered into the restaurant toward the back, where their favorite table overlooked an attractive pond.

The pond was lovely in all seasons, but at this time of the year, when the days were poised on the verge of a new spring season, it was especially picturesque. Birds were twittering and flying noisily about. Some perched on shrubs at the pond's edge and preened their feathers. Life is good, they might have been chirping, and the old woman, had she understood their language, would have agreed.

"Well, Beth?" The old woman invited her great-granddaughter to explain herself.

Beth looked across at her great-grandmother, and said, "Bobby and I are going on a cruise next week—that's why I had to move our luncheon up. It's a promotion put on by his company, and at the last moment, there was an extra stateroom, and Bobby was next in line to get it. Isn't that wonderful?"

Getting ready for a cruise in a single week required an art not everyone could master, but the old woman had little doubt that Beth would get her wardrobe and attitude in perfect readiness by the time the ship left the pier. Beth was so much like herself, the old woman thought, and she meant it as a compliment to both. She knew it was a talent, being able to handle abrupt changes with diplomacy and skill. *I think the term "roll with the punches" is what I mean*, she thought to herself.

Beth talked endlessly about the cruise she and Bobby would take out of New Orleans in eight days. The old woman appeared to be listening intently. This, too, was an art, for she found her mind wandering, often to the birds and scenery of the pond.

Beth often talked too fast for the old woman to follow. Many times she wanted to tell her grandchildren and great-grandchildren that they talked too fast, used too many unfamiliar expressions, or that their voices were either too loud or too soft.

Of course she never criticized any of them. Didn't they put up with her antiquated expressions, her oft-repeated stories, and her uneven voice that sometimes trailed off into small coughing spasms? She looked at Beth with fresh determination to follow with genuine interest what she was saying.

The old woman and her great-granddaughter enjoyed a perfect lunch, and by the time they had finished their key lime pie, Beth had calmed down considerably. "Grand," she asked, "do you remember when you and Granddad took your cruise?"

The old woman laughed aloud as she wiped her mouth. How could she ever forget that wonderful event in their lives?

Still, she smiled up at Beth and answered, "I think I remember every wonderful detail of it!"

It had only been two hours since she had left the rest home, but by the time the old woman and her wheelchair had been returned to her room, she felt as if she had been away for days. She wondered to herself if she was too infirm to tolerate these outings, but immediately disregarded the suggestion. She did not intend to miss the next luncheon invitation Beth extended, nor the chance to hear all about the cruise.

Beth and a nurse assisted her from wheelchair to bed, and after they left, the old woman settled down to her afternoon rest. Usually at this time she enjoyed a nap, but not today! Visions of the cruise she and her husband had taken kept her wide awake.

Their children had wanted the golden wedding celebration of their parents to be incredibly special, not the usual cake-and-punch reception at the church. She remembered protesting that such a reception would be just fine, perfectly suitable, and quite in line with the kind of people they had always been: ordinary folks, loyal to their church and community. But no, that sort of reception wouldn't do, the children insisted, and a month before the golden date, cruise tickets and an itinerary were presented to her and her husband. What's more, to create an absolutely impossible dream, there were tickets for their four children and their spouses, too! This would be the cruise of a lifetime, and indeed it was.

The old woman remembered that, although she and her husband were comparatively young for a couple celebrating fifty years of married life, they did not use the swimming pools and spas aboard the ship, nor did they participate much in the ship's nightlife. There were stage shows, musicals, dances, movies—goodness, what wasn't there available for those aboard? But they were content to sit in deck chairs and watch their grown children having the time of their lives.

They spent time in the ship's library, reading books and chatting with others aboard who were about their age. They also enjoyed walking around the deck and getting their exercise at a leisurely pace their bodies appreciated.

Most of all, however, what they truly enjoyed about the cruise was sitting at the large table in the ship's beautiful dining room, surrounded by their family. Every meal was perfect, and the smiling faces of their children produced a photograph etched on her mind … it never faded; it never grew old or tiresome.

The old woman had a talent for producing mental photographs that she could call up at will. It made her visits to the past a beautiful Technicolor event. The picture she now saw was one of herself and her husband, surrounded by their children. The picture was captioned with references to the great success they had enjoyed in the raising of their four children.

When the cruise ended, and life returned to more ordinary pursuits, she would recall visions of the ship and their family cruise. The gracious meals in the ship's dining room would play over and over again in her mind. These photographs added to the joy of her memories. Photographs and memories sustained her during uncomfortable times when illness or other aggravations interrupted the smooth sailing of her daily life. Some years later, after she lost her husband, she found herself dwelling more and more on this high-water event in their marriage.

Today Beth had asked if she could remember the cruise she had taken! Beth had not even been born the year of that cruise. So many things had happened since that cruise—the birth of great-grandchildren being some of the happier events. The love and respect her children had shown in providing their parents with such a glorious golden wedding celebration was a cherished memory, a perfect memory poised among others that continued to sustain her.

Here her thoughts inexplicably returned to the pond outside the window at the restaurant. Not for the first time, she thought what a wonderful thing a pond is. It serves as a transient home for many of God's migrating creatures. They would not stay long at the pond, but while they were there, it was their perfect habitat.

The old woman thought that people are transient creatures, too. They seldom stay put, but move from place to place as birds fly from climate to climate. She thought people should behave more like birds, fluttering about and carrying on great conversations with one another, enjoying one another's company. They were good travelers, these birds. She knew that being a good traveler was an art—an important one to master for people who wanted to see more of their world.

"I must remember to send a little card to Beth tomorrow. I will thank her for the lunch, but I want especially to wish her *bon voyage.* She will have the trip of a lifetime."

The old woman was happy to think about travel, but every bone she had protested that she had traveled enough for the day. She snuggled into her pillow for a pleasant afternoon nap.

April

Plans Ended by Storms
Become Blueprints for Beauty
Later in the Year

Always Young at Heart

In the flower garden, sunshine splashed interesting patterns on the brick walkway, over which the old woman's wheelchair rolled. She was delighted by the fragrance of the flowers and the bright green foliage; brighter because an April shower had washed them clean. From earliest childhood, she had loved the month of April. She never tired of remembering in great detail all the reasons why.

She had been an exuberant child, especially suited for playing out of doors the livelong day. In spite of her mother's warning to mind her manners, she flared into rebellion if bad weather forced her to remain indoors. April was the first month of the year when she could rely on a string of pretty days to safely run and play outside, so she always welcomed April and the return of spring. An observant child, she was familiar with all the signs of growth after a dormant winter.

She especially liked to see the baby chicks running after their mother hen. They looked nothing like their brown-feathered mother, but she knew the yellow down that covered them would give way to real feathers in a few weeks.

She knew their babyhood would pass quickly, even as she chased after the little fluffs of down and tried to mimic the *cheep, cheep* of their chicken small talk.

Beyond the chicken yard were blackberry brambles, and she liked to check the progress being made there. In a short time, the white blossoms would give way to small, hard green berries. These in time, would turn red, then a delicious black. It was her favorite berry, and to her mind, worth all the trouble it took to pick a syrup bucket full of them. Anyone could pick strawberries, but it took a real berry lover to get a pail of blackberries together. She knew her mother would bake a blackberry cobbler from the berries she picked, so she kept a close watch on the blackberry bushes. The opportunity for picking them demanded that she get to the berries before the birds feasted on them.

She also loved the wildflowers that grew in great profusion beyond the manicured lawn her parents maintained. These unbidden flowers returned each spring, and she picked large bouquets of them for her mother. Her mother would always put the flowers carefully in a pretty vase and set them on the kitchen table. Alas, the blooms soon drooped and faded, and the bouquet would be discarded. As she grew older, she thought the wildflowers were a perfect symbol for early spring. They were beautiful, untamed, and like herself, were better suited to the out of doors. Their season for providing enjoyment was brief. In a week or two, they faded and disappeared.

The April showers so responsible for this well-loved landscape were also over quickly. She remembered how much she loved to go outside after a shower and smell the clean fragrance of spring.

One of the things she especially liked to do was walk down the lane that led to the highway. On either side of this lane were tall trees that had been planted there many years ago by her father when he was not much more than a boy. The trees had grown quite tall, and their lower branches had been pruned so that the higher branches were easily seen. These branches reached across the lane toward one another, forming a natural cathedral ceiling. The girl liked to look upward at this heavenly ceiling and admire the lacy pattern formed by the early leaves of spring. At this stage in their growth, the leaves admitted a considerable amount of sky blue background, and she thought it the loveliest ceiling anywhere.

As the spring seasons came and went and the girl grew into young womanhood, her attachment to baby chicks, blackberry bushes, and the lacy new growth of trees did not fade. If anything, it intensified. Each April she knew she would revel in the renewal of life with all the rapture she had ever shown.

Another reason to love April was that it was often the time of Easter. She loved the entire season of Easter, whether in March or April, but she preferred the warmer air of April. She and her sisters would get new dresses, made by their mother, of course, which were always a pretty pastel color. The colors of Easter—pink, yellow, lilac, and green—mimicked the colors of the wild flowers that grew so gloriously in the fields where she loved to run and play.

April, year after year, represented a carefree and uncomplicated time for the girl; until that one year when the family became aware that a loved one would not be with them much longer. Her father's mother—her own much-adored grandmother—was very ill, and this time there would be no recovery.

This grandmother had been a heritage of strength and wisdom to the young girl. She had spent many happy days each summer with her grandmother and never tired of sitting at her side, listening to the stories the older woman shared. No rebel spirit urged her to run if she had the chance to sit beside her grandmother.

Now that she thought about it, her love of Easter had come from this grandmother. This grandmother planted all the tulips and other spring flowers in the beds that surrounded the property. This grandmother's chicken yard produced all those lovely little fluffs of yellow down. And standing beside this grandmother, she learned to pick the blackberries carefully to avoid the thorns.

The death of her grandmother that April might have spoiled the month forever, but something else occurred that produced a momentous change. She met and fell in love with the man she would marry. His calm, uncomplicated devotion was not unlike the strength she had felt in her grandmother. April had not deprived her of all comfort. It was a lesson to cherish: God never leaves us without a comforter.

As the years passed and moved the girl into the full blossom of womanhood, she may have given up the impulse to race through the meadows, gathering wild flowers, but she never lost her admiration for them. She was nostalgic always at the sight of baby chicks. April was still her month, and it continued to resurrect all her girlish enthusiasm.

She had always loved poetry, and was struck by these lines from Sir William Watson:

April, April
Laugh thy girlish laughter;
Then, the moment after,
Weep thy girlish tears.

She had shed tears enough in her life to appreciate the reference, but she was thankful that, even as the years passed, she still had the girlish laughter of her early April days. It kept her young at heart, and was an identifiable part of her personality, even as she grew into old age.

The years had brought any number of losses in her life. The passing of each loved one had diminished her considerably, especially that most grievous loss of all. She would miss him all the rest of her days. She sighed as she recalled a line from T. S. Eliot, "April is the cruelest month ..." April *was* cruel as it forced new life, "breeding lilacs out of the dead land, mixing memory and desire, stirring dull roots with spring rain."

The old woman looked again at the patterns on the brick walkway. They had changed since her last glance, because the sun had filtered its presence through different angles of growth. She considered the patterns, knowing that a force far beyond herself had produced them. It was the same force every year of her life that turned March into April. The force that produced a meadow full of flowers for her childish enjoyment. She was still a child at heart, never having lost her appreciation for the new life of April.

It occurred to her that the famous poet was right. There was a cruelty in the month. It was symbolized by the flowers that faded, the chicks that lost their down, and the spirited girl who ceased to run and play in the freedom of the meadows. The past seemed obscured by the power of the present.

A more benign spirit, however, eventually prevailed. The laughter returned; the spirit, like spring itself, reawakened to the detailed memories of all the accumulated Aprils. With her memories safely secure, the old woman breathed deeply the fragrance of a new spring.

Psalm to the Seasons

My soul praises you, God, for I perceive the beauty and balance of Your creation.
My eye beholds splendor, my ear detects the perfect rhythm of Your handiwork.
When my body is caught unaware in the snare of what my generation calls progress, my soul reminds me of Your world and Your perfect sense of proportion.

Then I am fed by reminiscences of unspoiled beauty:

Of the spring and lacy growth of new leaves on the trees; where trees line both sides of the road I travel, their arched boughs intertwine above my path in cathedral patterns, and remind me that Your dwelling place is where we look for You;

Of the soft and fragile perfection of young animals; the strong appeal of the young of all species reminds me that You renew continually Your creation; Your love sustains each new generation;

Of the ease and peace of summer, when it is possible to luxuriate in the warmth of Your generosity; the fullness of Your creation proves the reality of spring's promise;

Of green and growing meadows, alive with sound and smell and touch to assist the eye, whose blessing it is to behold it;

Of the autumn's orchard offering, which recalls Your command to be fruitful;

Of color, the sheer and soothing beauty, the warm and glowing strength of color to my soul. Thank You, God, for color, which reminds me of Your covenant with mankind;

Of lessons of purity observed in the winter snowfall; what a purifying cover I receive through forgiveness, obliterating the sin and decay inevitable in human life;

Of the evergreens that persist in winter bleakness to remind me that Your love favors no season; Your goodness extends throughout the year …

And from year to year …
May You be praised through souls
grown more sensitive through abundant appreciation
of Your goodness in creation.

Flowers from the Past

Today had been a wonderful time for the old woman in the wheelchair to treasure over and over. The wonder of the day began when she first awoke and realized she had slept very well. Others might say it's a simple thing, sleeping well. The old woman would tell them to reach an advanced age and endure the physical aches and pains she lived with all day long, then try to get a good night's sleep!

Because she awoke fully rested and feeling better than usual, she radiated smiles to everyone who entered her room. She was especially pleased that the good night's rest had been achieved without the help of pills or chants or special admonitions from anyone. She knew sleeping through the night was a blessing for older people, and it was a blessing she had been missing for quite a while.

When she felt good, many ordinary things fell into place easily and without complications. She was made ready for the day in much less time than usual, and she looked forward to her breakfast, because she had a good appetite and was hungry. Some mornings she only went through the motions of eating her breakfast. She was smiling this morning, and her happy expression was met with responsive smiles from others. All indications pointed to a happy day.

The old woman was off to a good start, and she knew exactly why it was important. Today was special: all four of her children were coming to the nursing home to have lunch with her. It was not her birthday or anniversary. She had to think a moment before she remembered that they were coming because all four of them were in town at the same time. That circumstance, like sleeping through the night, didn't happen often these years. Her children had children and grandchildren of their own, and their lives had splintered off in different directions. Two of her children lived in towns some distance away.

When breakfast was over, the old woman spent most of the morning looking out the large window that faced the parking lot. She looked at every arriving car, thinking it belonged to her children. Eventually her children appeared, and when they walked through the entry, she was right there to greet them. A lot of noisy laughter and kissing took place then. The old woman knew there was nothing more precious to her than the sight of her own four children.

Her son, one of the children who lived out of town, handed her a large group of irises. Her eyes misted over as she looked at these beautiful, graceful flowers. Always, in her family, they had been a favorite symbol of spring. That was only the beginning of the story of this bouquet, as the son began to explain.

"You know the history of these irises, don't you?" her son asked. The old woman was almost certain she did.

"They are the floral descendants of your own grandmother's garden!" he said as he leaned toward her wheelchair and placed the bouquet in her lap.

When she was a little girl, she spent many happy hours working alongside her grandmother in the flower gardens that bordered the house and property. Her grandmother had especially liked irises, jonquils, and tulips. She had called them "spring bulbs," and they magically appeared in full bloom about the time when everyone had given up on spring putting in an appearance. Other flowers in her garden, verbenas, petunias, and phlox, slipped in later and without much overture. But the spring bulbs! The old woman remembered they made a dramatic change in everyone's attitude when they burst into bloom. After a drab winter, these flowers found instant favor, for they were heralds of spring.

It took the girl many years before the irises became more than a featured image in her memory. She and her young husband made a drive back to the old home place. The house had long since been relocated, but the land itself was essentially the same as she remembered. Landmark trees helped the young woman explain the layout of the property to her husband. As she walked off the remembered places where the sidewalk and various flower borders had been, she was astonished to notice that there were irises everywhere. It was past their blooming season, but the unmistakable spikes of their leaves were healthy in spite of a generation of absence and neglect.

The irises, like the family itself, had multiplied each season. The young wife secured an implement from a neighbor, and her husband began to dig up clumps of irises. Even after enough plants had been removed to share with everyone in the family, there were enough remaining irises to satisfy the whole county.

Irises are sturdy flowers. They are not actually bulbs, but are produced from rhizomes, a fleshy root structure that sends up the spiky leaves and ultimately the flower. They are not temperamental like many bulbs are, nor are they demanding as, say, azaleas or roses. They are simply the perfect choice for a busy housewife who treasures pretty flowers.

Part of her grandmother's preference for irises was their dependability and their habit of blooming at Easter. Because her grandmother had cultivated irises, the granddaughter was also able to cultivate them. It was a point of family pride that her irises were grown from the very rhizomes from the very flower borders her own grandmother had planted.

In subsequent visits to the old home place, the woman dug up additional iris rhizomes. She presented boxes of rhizomes to her aunts who lived a great distance away. The aunts expressed delight and pleasure that their niece had grown into her heritage in a manner so reminiscent of their own mother. One of the lovable characteristics of their mother had been her practice of sharing.

The woman's son took pride in this passing on of the garden heritage, and he developed an impressive iris border at the back of his house. In the years when she was able to travel to his house, the old woman walked arm in arm with her son during the spring of each year to enjoy the splendid show of irises. Her son's children also loved the irises, and rhizomes had made their way to their homes as they developed their own gardens. Iris plantings were passed along to *their* children as these, her own great-grandchildren, became home-owners and developed flower gardens to beautify their property.

The old woman tried to add up all the generations that had enjoyed her grandmother's irises. She thought for sure there were six generations. Next, she tried to imagine how many iris plants there must be scattered all over Texas, New Mexico, and Oklahoma. These were the states where the generations succeeding her own had moved to. Knowing that an iris plant this year would be two plants the next growing season, she wondered how many thousands of iris plants were being enjoyed each year by gardeners who had never even known her grandmother.

Always she had credited this grandmother with instilling in her a steady, faithful trust in God. This grandmother had been a great source of wisdom and patience. As she made her way through the years, she would quote her grandmother and tell others about the blessing she had been, giving the grandmother a kind of earthly immortality, not unlike the irises she had cultivated.

Like the irises, opportunities for sharing grew and grew. The more she thought about it, those irises were the perfect symbol of her generous grandmother. They quietly produced without demanding a lot of care or attention. When they were in bloom, however, no one could deny the beauty and blessing they were to the place where they grew and flowered.

Today her son had brought so many irises to her that vases had to be retrieved from storage closets so bouquets of them could be scattered around the nursing home. She and her children had enjoyed a lovely luncheon in a private dining room. Her daughters had brought in some of her favorite things to eat, including a fresh coconut cake. They had enjoyed a wonderful visit, and everyone shared familiar stories about the family. These stories never lost their appeal, and no family reunion was complete without their being repeated.

The old woman had to sit very still in order to catch every word, and in spite of her best efforts to keep smiling, she would tear up from time to time. It was a wonderful visit with her children, and as always, she acknowledged the presence of her late husband by glancing up toward the ceiling from time to time, smiling as if she saw his rugged handsome features creased in a returning smile.

She thought the day ended all too soon, but as they hugged her goodbye, they promised to return tomorrow and every day during her son's visit in the area. The old woman knew it would tax her strength, but it was an expenditure of energy she was willing to give.

As the old woman settled into a late-afternoon nap, she began to recall more stories about her grandmother and the irises. She was sure she had never shared them with her children. Even if she had, she knew they would want to hear them. They were beautiful stories. These days she had a special urgency to relate the stories of family to her children, even if it meant some were repeated.

"The stories must be shared with the children before I forget them. After all, they are stories about faith, love, and generosity—and irises! It's their heritage!"

May

Celebrated Time
Month of Mostly Loveliness
Warms the Willing Heart

M Is for Memory

Where had the month gone? The old woman, sitting comfortably in her wheelchair, looked out upon the courtyard that had seemed bare only a few weeks ago. The flowerbeds were now choked with blossoms, and outlying shrubbery was puffed out with leafy growth. Trees beyond the courtyard were full of their own seasonal importance. The days and weeks had worked their transforming power in the month of May.

The old woman thought of the entire month of May as a symbol of life's many stages. Each stage demanded recognition—a celebration of its existence. She thought May had always been a month suitable for celebrations. Her earliest recollections included Mother's Day, and through the years, she had added the birthday and anniversary celebrations of many loved ones. These special days were scattered throughout the month. For many years, she was involved in the high-school graduations and proms of her children and grandchildren, all highly celebrated events. May was ripe with memories of it all.

These days the old woman's thoughts danced about a good bit, and she had difficulty getting traction on a line of thinking she wanted to pursue. She knew she was leaving out an important holiday. Finally it came: the end of May, when all across the country, Memorial Day celebrations were held. At her advanced age, this was the celebration that really mattered most. There were so many people whose memories she cherished, and she was glad a holiday had been declared to honor them. It was a good time, in the full bloom of a brand new spring, to think about all those spring times of childhood and early womanhood, of all the people who had made the years memorable.

She played with the letter *M* as she considered the impact of the month of May. Mother. Memorial. "*M* is for May and for Memory," she said aloud. These days, confined as she was to the wheelchair, she knew how important it was to keep her memory stimulated. Her travels into the past both entertained her and helped explain much of what she was experiencing in the present. Mostly, her memories were sweet; unspoiled by the mistakes she and others had made. She had a talent for picturing her memories as if they were little newsreels or albums of well-organized snapshots. It was a talent she had used over and over, and she knew it was responsible for giving her the reputation for having a sharp mind.

The memories this morning were crowding in, all of them associated with the month of May. There was the occasion when she was about five years old. Her mother had taken the children with her to visit friends. There were other children in the group; the old woman remembered five in all. The children were allowed to play outside while the adults enjoyed talking and visiting among themselves. The children were told to stay in the yard, but after a few minutes, they disobeyed and wandered beyond the lawn, down to the creek that ran behind the house. There they found blackberry bushes, and she remembered her small, five-year-old self thinking how much her mother loved blackberries. She began to pick them, as did the other children. They had no container to put the berries into, but, always being resourceful, she lifted the hem of her dress, creating a makeshift holder for the berries. When the children decided they had picked enough, they walked in triumph back to the house to show the adults how productive they had been.

Alas, her mother had not been pleased. The berries had produced a deep purple stain on the lovely pink fabric of the dress. The dress had been her Easter outfit that year, and featured smocking and embroidery that took more than a little extra effort of her mother's skill to produce. Now it was ruined, a fact her mother's tears made perfectly clear. How could such a wonderful gesture of generosity have turned out so completely wrong? The old woman remembered that it was many years before her mother could talk about the blackberry adventure with any degree of laughter or forgiveness in her voice.

She must have disappointed her mother many times over the years because of her willfulness. She recalled an earlier occasion when she was four. She and her younger sister played out on the lawn with their dolls and their playhouse, a little pup tent. Their mother was very busy with a new baby, so the girls were given strict orders to stay on the lawn.

A next-door neighbor had an assortment of garden ornaments, including colorful gnomes, scattered among her flowerbeds. The old woman remembered her small self gathering up the gnomes one at a time and moving them into the pup tent. They would serve as older brothers and sisters to her dolls. When the neighbor discovered her gnomes had traveled next door, she told the young mother what the little girls had done. The gnomes were returned, and the little girls were lectured. They were never to touch the gnomes again.

How do you explain that little four-year-old girl with the good memory who forgot her mother's instructions? That same afternoon, she carried the gnomes back into the pup tent. Again, she was ordered to return them to their flowerbed homes, and then she was punished. This little episode was repeated several times before the young child understood very clearly that moving the gnomes was not worth the effort. Either that, or she had moved on to some more interesting activity that did not involve gnomes, pup tents, or punishment.

Try as she might, the old woman in the wheelchair could not remember any other occasions when her younger self had deliberately disobeyed her mother. Mostly, she had been a good child, and she worked hard at pleasing her mother. Years of good behavior, however, failed to expiate these two remarkable examples of a willful child behaving badly. All the Mother's Day cakes she had later baked, the lovely dinners she had prepared, and the cards she had carefully selected for her mother failed to make the impression on her collected memories that the blackberry and gnome misadventures had.

The old woman knew it was a waste of time to dwell on these two early childhood misadventures, when the beauty of the moment was so much to be preferred. The day was full of bright sunshine highlighting the loveliness of the garden. Time now to think more about Memorial Day. She had so many friends and loved ones to think about. Her great joy these days was calling to mind the happy years when life was full of their presence.

Small wonder the old woman loved the month of May. Life well lived, was a continued celebration, and this was the month to take note of what made life sweet and good. Memorial Day was the very holiday perfectly scheduled for old people like herself. The tapestry of their lives was enriched by the design added to it by all those they loved and remembered.

The old woman was smiling as she turned from the garden to return to her room. In spite of their associations with her willfulness, she still loved blackberries. Blackberry jam was her favorite, and she read on the bulletin board that today's menu featured blackberry cobbler.

"Oh, I do love the month of May!"

Cobwebs

The human brain is a vast filing cabinet,
Its drawers filled with collected memories
Placed in no particular order.
The cobwebs of the past attach themselves
To folders intended to hold instructions
For the present.
Like jealous children, the cobwebs clamor
For attention to the extent that the brain
Can exercise little control over the
Order and arrangement of its filing system.
The insensitive call this senility.

The Letter

A letter was delivered to the old woman in the wheelchair as she sat in her room. She did not always get mail, but she received enough that it didn't surprise her. As she always did with her letters, she put it in the pocket attached to her wheelchair to be read later when her morning activities were completed.

It was her lifelong habit of reading mail in this delayed manner. This practice came from her paternal grandmother. That sainted woman used to talk with her during summer visits to the family farm, and she stored up all the wisdom to add sense and meaning to her own life as she grew into a young woman. That bit about the letters, for instance: her grandmother received precious few letters, and they were treasures to be enjoyed at leisure. Best not to rush such a rare blessing.

"When I get a letter from your mother," the young girl's grandmother explained, "I like to put it in my apron pocket and read it when my hard work is finished. I sit on the garden bench and rest a bit to catch my breath. Then I read the letter."

Ever after, the young girl remembered this habit of her grandmother's, and in fact, had largely adopted it as her own way to read mail, especially now that she was herself old and in the rest home. Some special things—like letters from loved ones—should be given their own special setting. She thought about this as she wheeled her way to the enclosed garden area where she most liked to read her mail.

The letter was from Amy, her youngest granddaughter. What a lovely young woman Amy had become. The old woman was puzzled. What has prompted this letter from Amy? It seems a bit early to be receiving a Mother's Day card, and it was nowhere near her birthday. Speculating on what could be the reason for Amy's letter preoccupied her as she entered the garden.

Settled at last, the old woman carefully opened the envelope. She could hardly believe her eyes as she read the news:

> Dear Grandmother,
>
> Joe and I are expecting a baby in a few months, and the ultra-sound indicates it will be a little girl. We want to name her after you. It is Joe's idea as much as mine—you have always been so kind and loving to him, that in fact it is his special wish. We just think that the next generation should have a little girl who bears your name. Let us know if you agree and approve.

The old woman felt tears spring to her eyes. She knew Amy and Joe had wanted children, but until now, it seemed they would not have any. But now a baby was on the way, and they wanted to name it for her! Life is remarkably strange and thrilling, the old woman thought to herself.

And that sweet Joe! She well remembered when Amy was going out with Joe, and how much her parents disapproved of him. The old woman had been ashamed of her own daughter—Amy's mother—and her son-in-law for being so pretentious and stuffy with their presumed importance. "Joe is just not suitable," her daughter said bitterly. She began the long litany of things wrong with Joe: wrong church, wrong relatives, wrong, wrong, wrong.

Amy and Joe, however, were not to be deterred, and when no approval from Amy's parents seemed forthcoming, they drove to a neighboring state and were married there. They called back home to alert everyone that they had married. The old woman's daughter came over to her house and cried bitterly that she had lost her daughter forever. The old woman provided what comfort and counseling she could, but it was her daughter's personal problem of attitude, and it was one her daughter had to solve herself.

When the young couple returned to the area, they were reluctant to visit Amy's parents, so they called at Amy's grandmother's house. They received a warm and loving welcome—the old woman had always liked Joe. She liked his family, too. Joe's father had done landscaping work in the neighborhood for many of her friends. She knew Joe's family were hardworking, honest people. She hugged Amy and Joe to herself and immediately began planning a reception for them. All the family on both sides must be invited. Amy looked at her grandmother with misgiving, but there was no mistaking the determination in her grandmother's voice. The date was set, the names of Joe's family were added to the list of Amy's family, and shortly after that, invitations were sent out.

It was a beautiful Sunday in late spring when the dinner reception was given. The old woman had seen that lovely tables were set outside on the lawn where the dinner would be served. She ordered small centerpieces for each table from her friend, the florist. Several family members had helped prepare the food. She well remembered that Joe's father had come by the week before and volunteered to make the garden setting perfect for the occasion.

"My, oh my," she asked herself, "is there a better word than perfect?" That garden was so exquisite, so bursting with blooms and greenery, that it even eclipsed the lovely tables with their charming centerpieces.

When all the family had arrived, everyone was quite surprised at how lovely Grand's garden was. How had she managed to do this in so short a time? Grand just smiled at Joe's father and nodded in his direction. As he seemed preoccupied with blushing, she explained, "Joe's dad did all of this. He understands how important variety and a tender touch are to a garden. That's why you do not see a constant display of one variety of flowers, like rows of corn, but a blending and shaping of different varieties. Makes my garden so much more beautiful." Everyone heartily agreed.

The great success of the party was etched in her memory by one beautiful scene: her daughter bending over some of the flowers, talking to Joe's father about the art of arranging a flowerbed. It was strange to say, and almost unbelievable, but from that moment, friendship and family had blossomed.

The old woman often recalled this wondrous change of direction in the lives of her daughter and son-in-law and their children. It had especially been a blessing for Joe and Amy. Now the blessing would include a precious baby girl in a few months, and it would bear her own name!

She had never been very fond of her name, and was not surprised that until now no one had seem inclined to name a baby after her. However, she must rethink her attitude toward her name: the new baby would be sharing it with her!

She remembered a line from Shakespeare: "What's in a name? That which we call a rose by any other name would smell as sweet." She frowned to place the line, then smiled to herself. "Ah yes, it's from *Romeo and Juliet.*"

June

Popular Month
Extolled by Poets
Preferred by Brides
Welcomed and Cheered
By Students and Teachers

June Bugs and Genies

The old woman in the wheelchair was moving about the garden, glad to have her chair's motorized wheels enabling her to reach every corner she wanted to visit. The garden was especially beautiful in June, and she said a little prayer of thanksgiving for the caretakers who maintained it.

As she leaned toward a bed of flowers, she spotted a June bug. Then another. She could remember from her years as a gardener that June bugs were pests, and in this stage of their life cycle, they ate plants. Not one of her favorites of God's creations, the June bug.

She paused. *Now where did that thought come from?* She had begun to think about a little boy who lived in her neighborhood when she was a small girl. *His nickname, can you believe it, was June Bug! Did I ever know his real name? For the life of me, I can't recall it.* June Bug was a lively youngster who seemed to get along well with everyone. Before she could learn much about the boy with the interesting nickname, he and his family moved away.

In our lives, people come and go, rather like the flowers in this lovely garden. She was thankful for each and every person—at least right now she *thought* she was thankful for each one—

whose life had intersected hers through the years. "People make all the difference!"

She laughed to think that the only creature listening to her was the mockingbird chirping a response from the crepe myrtle on which it perched at the edge of the garden. And, of course, the June bugs who had stimulated her thinking.

Gardens often made her think about her grandmothers and the wisdom they had passed along to her. Her paternal grandmother was especially wise, and enjoyed her company when they sat on the back porch, peeling peaches or snapping peas. These were their special times.

One summer afternoon as they sat hulling black-eyed peas, her grandmother explained her idea of how to anticipate an expected pleasure.

"I like to finish a bit of work before I stop for a glass of iced tea and my new magazine. If I am in the garden, I work my way down the rows until I reach my garden bench. Then the tea, or a letter in my apron pocket, will give me greater pleasure."

Many times through the years, she would remember her grandmother's bit of wisdom. In the several locations where she had moved, she always liked to place a bench in some sheltered, remote location as homage to this grandmother. She often contrasted her grandmother's willingness to anticipate a pleasure patiently with the way people today demanded instant gratification. If she could wish away this unattractive modern practice, she would.

Okay, I'll pretend that some genie has granted me three wishes. I have already made one. What should the other two be?

She thought of her other grandmother, the one who was so clever and funny. While neither grandmother had been blessed with a comfortable life because times were hard back then, neither really complained—especially this grandmother, who could turn gray skies and rainy days into celebrations. She could take the humblest food, and with clever designs and combinations present a luncheon plate that even finicky eaters like herself and her little sisters would eat with great pleasure. "Use your imagination," this grandmother encouraged.

How many little drawings and early poems and stories did I produce because this grandmother encouraged me to use my imagination?

Making something out of nothing is a talent, and this grandmother knew how to create from thin air an atmosphere where every child was important and every day full of blessings.

That would be my second wish, I think, that everyone would do something useful with her imagination—make a happy day out of a dreary one; create a charming luncheon out of plain food; create fun and pleasure instead of complaining about everything.

By now she was fairly caught up in the pleasant activity of the imaginary genie who had granted her three wishes. Where would she go for the third wish; which person in her past would inspire her thinking? It just seemed natural to think about her grandfather, the one who belonged to the grandmother with all the wisdom. He had wisdom, too, she remembered, and both of them were a strong, inspiring presence in her early life.

Children with wise and loving grandparents have been singled out by God for wonderful blessings.

This grandfather loved to have his grandchildren visit. His dry wit and energetic lifestyle made an impression on them. A kid would find it hard to sit around, doing nothing all day when visiting this grandfather. He inspired them to work alongside him, and those who did learned a lot about the value of work.

She remembered one time after all the chores were done, that watermelons were cut open and placed on a large table out to the side of the house. She had always loved watermelon; it was the treat she looked forward to every summer when she stayed with her grandparents. On this occasion, perhaps too many watermelons were cut. The others had left for the house, and only she and her grandfather remained with several untouched slices of watermelon.

"You really like watermelon, don't you, Granddaddy?" her young self had asked.

"Not really," he replied. "I just don't want it to go to waste."

Poor Granddaddy, she thought, having to eat all the remaining watermelon because the others had left it behind. She looked into his blue eyes, which were twinkling to match the grin on his face. Like all his humorous expressions, this one took a while to sink in, but when it did, she knew the two of them shared an open secret: they both loved watermelon.

After they finished eating the watermelon slices, they cleaned up the table and headed to the house. She held her grandfather's hand as they walked toward the back porch. She looked up at her granddaddy's wrinkled, sunburned face and felt deeply comforted. He had always found the simplest ways to make her feel loved and special. It seemed to be part of his generous and charming personality.

If recalling this precious moment from her girlhood was to become a third wish, how might it be expressed?

"Actually, that's easy. I would wish that every child could enjoy the love of grandparents, and that every child would know the experience of being very special.

"It would be a better world if my three wishes would come true. They're not that far beyond possibility. All it would take is for all those blessed with grandchildren to take time to share with them their wisdom, their charm, their love and interest. That would cure many of the world's ills. It would be the saving grace of today's children."

The old woman said this last bit aloud in the direction of the mockingbird. The bird cocked its head to the side as if indicating complete agreement.

She thought she should give action to her thoughts, as she often did, by returning to her room and placing a phone call or two. She intended to call several of her great-grandchildren. She needed to see how they were enjoying their summer vacation, and more importantly, they needed to know she cared enough to inquire.

A small thing, surely, but maybe several generations down the road each of them will recall a great-grandmother who loved them, and was interested in how they were spending their summer.

As she made her way inside, she heard the clap of thunder – a summer shower? Or applause from some sainted grandparents from the edge of heaven sending their approval?

Birthdays

June, the silvery moon we happily
Sang to on the hayrides of youth
Or the barefoot saunters on the beach

Is now more distant, a fading wisp
Of light among the stars, and,
Like them, far beyond our reach.

But now we sing, our voices thin,
To celebrate the passing years,
And blow the lighted candles from the cake.

I puff and blow a hundred moons
Of light while Happy Birthday shouts
Proclaim a silvery journey I could make.

The Road

The old woman kept a small bookcase in her room. Its space did not allow for all the books she had treasured through her life; she thought that might have required a regular library. The three shelves of this bookcase did allow for two or three translations of the Bible, her Complete Works of Shakespeare, books by C.S. Lewis, and several volumes of poetry. Other books on the shelves came and went, but these she could not part with.

With a sigh, she closed the volume of Robert Frost's poems. She had read, perhaps for the thousandth time, "The Road Not Taken." Recently she had taken note of a modern interpretation of the poem that threw into a cocked hat all she had ever been taught about what Frost meant. She was quite happy with her own understanding and interpretations. She didn't like for modern writers to suggest she had it wrong. They also took aim from time to time with the literature she loved. "Why don't they write their own material and leave the rest alone," she said aloud to no one.

She had always thought the poem spoke about the enchantment of choices. Every life has intersections where decisions must be made, providing an altered direction for a person. If a person took the trouble to trace the pivots made and subsequent directions they brought about, it could be argued that all decisions are exercises of fate.

That's a little heavy, the old woman told herself. "I can think of a few decisions that simply produced momentary joy, not earth-shaking changes in direction."

She maneuvered from her wheelchair to her bed and settled down to think about choices, going as far back into childhood as she could manage. This was one of her favorite activities, anyway, and she especially enjoyed reliving her early years if she had a question to settle.

It didn't take her long to choose a road from her own childhood to direct her thinking. She had always known this road, for it led to the hill on which stood the house where she was born. After her parents moved from the area, the house and land were leased by her grandparents, so her visits there continued.

"I suppose I could write a poem about that place," she said to herself, "but I'd rather just think about it in really simple terms that no would-be revisionist could mistake. If I were to write it out as a description, here is what I would say:"

"'The most treasured geography of my childhood was the road that led to grandmother's house. At its top, this rural part of East Texas enclosed a neighborhood of six houses. Children lived in most of them, so my brother and I had playmates when we visited. Beyond the hill, wooded land framed this idyll, which provided the safest of playgrounds for children.

"'The hill's steep incline invited deeds of derring-do. With roller skates, wagons, or bicycles, we raced recklessly to its bottom, where a wooden bridge rattled pleasantly as we crossed it, slowing our speed before the upward incline that led to the highway and Charley's Filling Station.

"'The tar road contrasted with the orange-red clay soil of the hill. No East Texas child who has ever played on a rural tar road can forget its aroma or the misery it inflicted in the heat of summer when a bare foot missed a bike pedal and touched the sticky substance. We didn't tell our parents, but we liked to find a pure patch of tar and scrape beneath its surface to extract a wad to chew. It tasted awful, but all of us kids tried it at least once.

"'At the wood bridge there were three choices."

See? My road had choices, too.

"'We could labor up the shorter incline to the filling station, but we only did this if we had a nickel to buy a cold soda. We seldom had a nickel in our pockets, so we considered the second choice. We could lay our skates or bike by the side of the road and walk in the creek bed. This shallow stream was always clear, and if it was summer and we had been barefoot, the water was a relief to our stone-bruised, clay-encrusted feet.

"'In May, blackberry bushes encroached upon the stream, the plump berries tantalizing us until our hands and mouths were stained a rich purple. In June, a plum tree further downstream provided tart refreshment. In July we raided the possum grape vines. In October there were persimmons to pick.

"'Whatever season—although summer was always our favorite—the creek provided a palette of color through its bank of wildflowers and foliage of pine, live oak, sweet gum, and cedar trees.

"'In winter, pine and cedar were especially fragrant and green, so we would gather clumps to take to grandmother so that she could use them to decorate the house and dining table.

"'The stream bed itself was a rich field to mine for smooth colorful rocks. All of us had slingshots, and these rocks were perfect for our arsenal."

My grandkids will want to know what the third choice was.

"'The third choice was the one we made most often: we could turn around and trudge back uphill so we could race down it again! Our happy shrieks echoed over the hillside, and for the life of me, I do not recall that anyone was ever hurt. No Band-Aids or antibiotic creams were needed, even if any were to be found in grandmother's spare medicine cabinet. Our blisters were badges of honor, and they all healed in time. Modern day skateboarders would have loved the challenge of our hill.

"'The sun beat down unmercifully on our little towheads, but we would huff and puff our way back uphill for the privilege of sailing down it again and again. Only when the sweat dripped down our faces in dusty streaks that would nearly blind us—only when a glass of ice water seemed more desirable than another race downhill would we head for grandmother's house."

The old woman was now lost in a haze of endless trips up and down the road of her childhood. Soon she would be asleep, and like as not, she would dream sweetly of the road that held no bad choices.

There were other intersections in her life that had made a difference. She knew what choices these intersections provided, and she was content with the difference they had made in her life. The family she treasured came from the choice she made in marriage, and she could not imagine what kind of road her life would have navigated had she chosen a different life mate.

"Don't even want to think about it," she said. "I'd much rather think about skating down the tar road again. This time, though, it would be nice to have a nickel in my pocket."

July

Celebrate the Fourth!

Stars and Stripes, Forever March!

Flags, Fly High Unfurled!

Just over Half

The old woman was carefully helped from her daughter's van and placed in her wheelchair. She had been gone two days, and she was exhausted. Every bone in her body protested against such adventures.

She had been taken to a funeral in a town about a hundred miles away. Ordinarily she would have been satisfied to wire flowers, send a card, or make a telephone call. This was no ordinary funeral; this was the service marking the passing of her oldest nephew. She would be unable to live with herself had she not attended. Her daughter agreed to see to her safe transport, and so it was that she was able to attend the funeral of her nephew.

She and her daughter stayed overnight with her old friend who lived in the area with her own daughter. The visit had been something to treasure, and it made the funeral trip less sad. It had been several years since she and her old friend had been able to see each other.

July shouldn't be for funerals, she complained as she was helped to her room. July is for celebrations, like birthdays. Even the birthday of our country is on the Fourth. It's too hot in July to attend funerals and get all sweaty from the heat and the tears. These were her weary thoughts as she entered her room. "I much prefer celebrations," she muttered to herself.

Her earliest recollections of July were about the country's birthday. She could remember visiting her grandparents on the Fourth at the family farm. Also visiting were every aunt and uncle and cousin in the family. Her granddaddy had bought cases of cold drinks—they were not in cans or large liter bottles then, but neat, small bottles—and he had made sure to have an assortment. He had selected from his watermelon patch several of the largest to have on hand for those who shared his love of summer's favorite slice. Her grandmother baked several cakes, at least one of them devil's food, thick with chocolate frosting—her favorite.

July 4 was a natural halfway point in the year that headed toward Christmas. It was the only holiday during the summer that the extended family celebrated, and for many, it was their favorite. They liked the pace of summer; the lazy loafing about and the incredibly refreshing water of the creek that ran its course at the bottom of the hill.

There were wide spots in the creek that were deep enough for the children to swim. They splashed about in great abandon while their grandmother and aunts assembled an outdoor picnic. Yes, July started out with a great bang, literally! Her granddaddy always managed to get a few small firecrackers for each child, and of course, sparklers. These were carefully saved until it was dark enough to admire their display of fiery sparks.

July was a month of family birthdays, too. A sister, a brother, at least two aunts, and—oh my, she reflected, this old friend of mine. "I must remember to get her card in the mail tomorrow. It can serve double-duty, as I must thank her for being able to stay overnight."

The July birthdays in her family were scattered from July 10 through July 31. Always, parties were planned, and fancy cakes were baked.

July was just a perfect month for celebrations, and as a young girl, she had thought July Fourth was the kickoff for an entire month of cake and ice cream, swim parties and picnics; all happy celebrations.

Celebrations were designed to be happy occasions, and the old woman was enthusiastically in favor of them. "We can never get enough happiness; we need all we can get a hold of to overcome sad events, like funerals," said the old woman to herself, wincing not only at the discomfort of moving from wheelchair to bed, but in being reminded that she had just returned from a funeral. "I much prefer birthdays."

Birthdays celebrate that memorable moment of actual birth. She well remembered when her little brother was born. Her daddy had driven her over to her grandmother's house, where her young aunts would care for her. Her grandmother would be with her mother during the birth of the baby. She remembered looking up at her daddy's face and seeing a mixed expression of joy and concern that she was unable to understand. Later in the evening, when he arrived to collect her for the return drive, the concern was gone, and his face was radiant with joy.

"You now have a baby brother," he said as he laughed and hugged her to him. "You will love him."

Indeed, she did love that little brother, from the first moment she saw his little red face nestled close in her mother's arms.

There were numerous other babies born in the extended family during those years of her childhood, but no birth was as memorable or as precious to recall as this one. Partly, she thought, because it was the earliest she remembered, and partly because her daddy had used great sensitivity in drawing her into the drama of her little brother's birth. Each July as the family celebrated his birthday, she took a proprietary interest in helping to plan the party. "It's what big sisters do," she told everyone in her most important voice.

Birthdays are rites of passage as we move, uncertainly at times, but hopefully with faith and assurance, toward that final rite of passage, the funeral. The old lady was not happy with the way her mind kept returning to the subject of funerals. She was determined to think about the old friend she had enjoyed visiting. That kind of thinking would enable her to go to sleep and have pleasant dreams.

They had been friends since both were ten years old and classmates in the same schoolroom. They enjoyed a lot in common. Being oldest in each of their families was just a circumstance, but they also both loved to read and enjoyed learning—now that was the stuff that made young people friends forever. And so they had been, from then and throughout their lives.

This friend's birthday was in July, and many times her family would plan a trip to the beach to celebrate it. She would always be invited along. It was almost like a replay of the July Fourth party her grandparents hosted. There were lots of people, lots of food, and lots and lots of water to splash about in.

She thought about the ocean's water: the relentless movement of the waves toward the shore, and then the steady, predictable movement back into the depths from which it had come. Life is like that. We are like the waves. We move toward the shore of life and activity, and enjoy the celebration of whatever it is our time to spend there. Then, at the time when the Creator who controls the waves determines, our wave of life returns. Although we have been given control over much of our existence, there is an ultimate control that we bow in reverence to, and our place is to obey. When we live in perfect obedience to that control, life should be one of continued and beautiful celebration.

The old woman liked the way she had been able to move beyond the exhaustion and sadness of the funeral to reflect on the peace and joy that are available to those who live in harmony with their Creator.

"I am no longer overcome with sadness. I may be weary, but not to the middle of my bones," she said. "God has given me peace, and I expect that I will be able to rest well." She turned off her bedside light and moved into the familiar comfort of her pillows.

Waves of Love

The rays of dawn had reached the sea
When I stood there and looked afar
Upon the vast and rising deep,
Beyond where sky and water meet,
To gaze upon the one remaining star.

On yellow sand, I watched the waves
Toiling toward their goal of reaching shore.
Their energetic pounding
Was joyful in resounding,
Recreating motion created long before.

A shiny plant had washed ashore
And lay before me at my feet,
All glistening there and shiny bright,
Its greenness gave me fresh insight
About life's journey each of us repeats.

Relentlessly the waves moved on.
I firmly stood there on the shore
And marveled at the seaside's glory,
Proclaiming daily Creation's story
In ways I'd not considered heretofore.

I turned to see the brightening sun
Whose warmth had lightened sky above.
My footsteps printed in the sand,
I felt a part of God's own plan
This morning as I watched His waves of love.

Nadine

It's just a fact. The old woman in the wheelchair was in a sad but reflective mood. *The older we get, the more people we miss. They have already made that journey to eternity, and we are left to mourn their loss.* Every day, it seemed, the old woman spent time reflecting on the life of a departed friend or loved one. Today she found her thoughts continually going to Nadine, then realized it was the one-year anniversary of her death.

Nadine, a decade older than herself, had first been a close friend of her oldest daughter. However, when her daughter brought the two women together at a luncheon, an instant friendship sprang up and blossomed. The friendship had begun several years before Nadine became a resident at the nursing home. She and her daughter made it a habit to visit Nadine each week there. It was never considered a burden, but rather something they enjoyed doing together. Adding to the pleasure of their visits was all the news they had to exchange, because the three women had many friends in common. Plus, Nadine had charming stories to tell about her girlhood, and she loved to share them.

That's the way it is with old people, the woman in the wheelchair admitted. *We have accumulated so many stories, and we have rehearsed them so often in our minds that we can relate them to others without changing a word. Nadine's stories were perfect little vignettes—easy to follow and remember.*

The old woman and her daughter especially liked the story Nadine often told about the time she and her sisters encountered trouble as they walked to school. Three little girls with book bags on their backs that weighed almost as much as they did had an additional burden. The middle sister was mentally handicapped, and often the victim of slurs shouted at her by thoughtless schoolmates.

One day Nadine and her older sister removed their book bags from their backs and used them as weapons to swing at the cruel children who had tormented their helpless sister. When they arrived home from school later that day, they went into their father's office to report what they had done. That gentle soul, a Methodist minister, listened to their account, then shook his head and advised, "Rise above it, girls, rise above it."

The old woman in the wheelchair often wondered how many times through her life Nadine had found occasion to "rise above it, rise above it." Nadine was a tiny little person, ever frail, but her loud, authoritative voice demanded respect. Somewhere along the way of "rising above it" she had developed vocal skills to intimidate anyone who would threaten her comfort or safety.

Nadine kept on her bedside table the books important to her, and she read them over and over. Foremost among them was the Bible, whose well-marked pages indicated the verses she found especially inspiring. She was counselor on the spot to anyone who came into the room with a problem. Her habit of quoting chapter and verse to everyone may have been disconcerting to a few, but there were some whose lives were changed by the wholesome influence of Nadine's caring concern. More than one on the staff gave her credit for helping them correct problems in their lives.

Nadine was easily irritated at the casual attitude the modern world had of marriage. She told and retold the time a cleaning woman dusted the dresser in her room and looked at the framed portrait of Nadine's late husband. "Is this your husband?" she asked indifferently.

"Yes," Nadine answered. "He was my husband for sixty years." This was spoken in a voice of soft tenderness, not her usual authoritative tone.

Expecting a favorable remark or something like it, Nadine was shocked when the cleaning woman laughed harshly and replied, "Sixty years with the same man? I couldn't stay that long with *any* man."

Why Nadine took such exception to the woman's thoughtless observation was puzzling, but it obviously bothered her. Her regular visitors were aware of the hurt, for she told and retold the incident. The old woman in the wheelchair remembered her own daughter remarking, "I want to tell Nadine, rise above it, girl, rise above it."

When the old woman herself became a resident in the nursing home, Nadine had been there for almost a decade, and she was well acquainted with the routine. Part of the old woman's rather easy adjustment to life in the nursing home was owed to the friendly assistance Nadine provided. By then Nadine had developed the habit of telling anyone who would listen, "I don't know why I am still alive, why I am still here. What more is there for me to do?"

Her rhetorical question had no easy answer, and yet the old woman in the wheelchair observed that Nadine fulfilled a useful mission. For one thing, she had a regular stream of visitors. Because the two women knew so many people in common, the visits were often to both of them, and they developed into virtual parties. These occasions were filled with laughter and happy exchanges of friendly news. Visits intended for ten minutes laughed themselves into half an hour, and everyone seemed uplifted when the party ended and the visitors went away.

The old woman decided that these visitors, like the individuals who had been spiritually guided by Nadine's wisdom, were evidence that even at this advanced age, life still had purpose.

Unusual among Nadine's visitors were some young students. They had adopted her as one of their church youth activities, and their interest in her continued long after they had completed their project. Snapshots of them in their school uniforms, then in prom gowns, were tacked to her bulletin board. When they left the area for various colleges, their cards and letters to her arrived with regularity. These were shared with those who visited Nadine. When the girls were home on holidays, they always stopped by to visit their old friend.

For her part, Nadine's interest in them was reciprocal, and her conversations with friends often included references to "her girls." Anyone whose visit to Nadine coincided with one of the visits the girls continued to make could feel the sweet bond of friendship they had forged with one so many generations beyond their own.

Why was Nadine still living; what purpose had she to serve? Indeed, all a person had to do was list the names of those whose lives continued to intersect her own. When Nadine's time finally ran its course, she left behind a number of people who were stronger or more confident because she had been their friend and counselor.

Small wonder I miss this remarkable friend. The old woman was still sad in her reflections as she wheeled herself in the direction of her room.

Perhaps the sadness increased the difficulty she usually had in making the transition from wheelchair to bed. She had to give extra consideration to her aches and pains as she made the effort.

She smiled at the spectacle she knew she must have been making. *Rise above it, girl, rise above it.*

August

Roller Coasters of Golden Grain

Undulate across the Land

Pantries Will Be Filled

Oreo

The old woman often wondered how life differed in other nursing facilities. Some had told her that one place was pretty much the same as another. Since her experience both before and after being admitted to this one was limited, she had no way of knowing—until yesterday, that is.

Her oldest daughter had returned from a visit to another state to visit her husband's relatives. Several family members were in a nursing home, and one of them celebrated her hundredth birthday. The big reunion was well attended; relatives came from great distances to see one another. Not all who came were relatives. One of the visitors was a black-and-white cat, Oreo. The story of Oreo fascinated the old woman, and she had her daughter repeat the details.

The residents in that nursing home longed for a pet cat, and the activities director, who lived on a farm at the edge of town, brought in a kitten from the last litter born to one of the barn cats. This little kitten, with its mostly black fur highlighted with white feet and underbelly, received the name of Oreo. The kitten adjusted to its new home as resident pet and roamed the hallways at will. For many of the residents, the obliging kitten was a soft, cuddly creature that satisfied a deep need. There may have been a few residents who didn't care for cats, but Oreo could identify them easily and be depended on to keep his distance.

From the beginning of his residency at the nursing home, Oreo was attracted to Tillie, the mother-in-law of the activities director. Tillie not only loved kittens, but she had lived on that same farm where Oreo had been born. Nurses and visitors alike remarked at the decided affection the small cat had for Tillie and wondered if it had anything to do with the farm. They noted that visitors to the farm who later called at the nursing home were given the same studied attention by Oreo. It seemed he made a beeline to Tillie's room when someone called, and then proceeded to examine every square inch of the visitor's clothing before jumping into her lap to be stroked. Did he get a whiff of his origins?

From time to time, stories appear about those who claim they can communicate with animals and read their minds. What would such a gifted person be able to learn about Oreo? This talkative cat would probably communicate this:

I know it was a good thing to be removed from that litter at the farm, but at the time, it was the only life I knew, and I missed terribly the opportunity to snuggle up to my mother with all my siblings. We were getting too old to be depending on our mother so much, and she spent more and more time away from us, pursuing her job of catching mice in the barn. During her absence, we cuddled up to one another in a shared dependence.

My siblings and I seemed destined to follow the same hard life of our parents. The life of a barn cat is wild and unpredictable.

At the time, however, it was all I knew, so I was unsettled when I was taken from all that was familiar to me and placed in the nursing home. There were no other animals there, and at first I was very lonesome.

I later learned that my sadness of dislocation was an emotion shared by the residents.

I longed for the sight or smell of something familiar to me. I would hang around the office of the activities director because she was the one who brought me here, and I liked the farm smell she brought each day with her to the nursing home. It was the smell of home. Gradually I became adjusted, and quickly learned which of the old people at the nursing home enjoyed my company. I chose to spend most of my time hanging around their rooms.

I would hear the staff explain to visitors, "If you don't want the cat around, just brush him off." Very few people did. I think many of them liked me because I was a diversion. In the stressful atmosphere of a visit with an aged loved one who maybe doesn't even remember who you are, a little distraction like a friendly cat can be a real relief. I began to think of myself as a blessing, and my friendly manner won me lots of affection. Funny thing: I was being given credit for adding something special to the atmosphere of the home, and all the time, the home was providing something special to me, a sense of being important.

It was obvious that among all the residents at the nursing home, I preferred Tillie. For one thing, she loved soft kittens, and she made no bones about that. For another, many of her visitors—and she always had many of them, because she was from a big family who loved her very much—had come straight from the farm. I could detect the smell of my original home about them, and it gave me a sense of comfort. Tillie's visitors greeted me with affection, and they liked me to be in the room; not because they wanted a diversion, but because they also liked warm, cuddly cats.

It was something about the old people that I picked up on quickly. They like the hugs and touches of affection and seem to yearn for more of them. I suspect that this is something from their life before residential care that they miss most. Some of the old people in the home have little stuffed animals on their beds or atop their television sets. More than once, I have seen them hug these little stuffed animals and coo at them as they would to a small child. You don't have to be smart as a cat to figure this out, and I wish every room had a cuddly stuffed animal in it.

Let me be frank, though. None of those cute little stuffed bears can do the job I do. When I jump on the lap of a resident, I purr as loudly as I can. I also rub my head against the ribcage of the patient until I can hear their heartbeat. It's a healthy sound, and I know my presence has something to do with its steady rhythm of contentment. Sometimes I settle down for a pleasant nap while the person on whose lap I am snuggled into watches a television program, reads her mail, or takes her own nap.

My job at the nursing home beats chasing mice across the rafters of a barn. I will probably live more than my allotted nine lives in this safe place, compared to the brief lifespan of a barn cat. Already, I have been here several years, and from my kittenhood, when I was just a fluff of fur, I have grown into a sleek creature of some consequence. It pleases me that 95 percent of the people who walk through the front door know who I am. The other 5 percent look at me with curiosity, wondering what a cat is doing in a facility like this.

I could tell them a few things about curiosity, but that hits too close to home for a cat, so I would settle for the chance to say this to them:

Give your loved one a big hug – and don't be so brief with it!
Drop by more often, and don't be in such a hurry to leave.
Massage their hands, then kiss those beautiful old gnarled hands. They grew gnarled tending to you.
Throw your arms around them during the visit; let them relax in the presence of your warmth.
Don't be upset if they seem to forget who you are. You are of great importance to them, and so is your visit. They will remember the visit in their own way, in their own time.
Give me more than a passing hug, too—it will be an activity you can share with them. They know me very well, and will be pleased to see you join in.
You might take time to thank me. I'm just a cat, but I am performing a great service. So is the staff—thank them, too!

I imagine there are duplicates of me in nursing homes all over the country. Perhaps in some facilities, my place is filled by a dog or a cage of beautiful singing birds. We are gifts of the animal world to the limited existence of those who must now reside in nursing homes. I am proud of my career. Beats the mice routine, paws down.

The old woman in the wheelchair was startled from her nap. She had dreamed she had been holding a soft, cuddly cat, and its purring sound of contentment had been a great comfort. A noise in the hall had caused it to leap from her chair and disappear from her room. She could remember that the cat had talked to her in a very confidential way about his years of service. She reached for the phone to dial her daughter's number.

"You'll never guess who just paid me a visit!"

Rest

The farm has gone to bed,
Its charges all accounted for,
Its prayers all sweetly said.

Only a distant echoing sound
Intrudes from far away—
The farm has settled down.

Teeming once with life and toil,
It forged a pact from those it owned
To wrest a living from the soil.

It now sets free all those it fed
And welcomes back its natural self.
The farm has gone to bed.

There's a Louse on the Bonnet!

There is something unique about the month of August. The old woman was pondering the month's special quality as she wheeled herself toward the rest home's dining room. Every August she could remember served as a mood-setter for the remainder of the year. No other month seemed to have that cornerstone quality. August fulfilled the promise of summer by providing uninterrupted days of blazing heat. At the same time, August heralded the coming autumn's more benign season by providing cooler, more pleasant evenings. She always loved the quiet and peace of August evenings.

People, too, have a double-faced feature in their makeup. Like August, they have a kind of hot-and-cold personality. She considered the three tablemates she would encounter in the dining room. New seating assignments for the noon meal had been in effect for the last several days, and she was unable to warm up to her new tablemates. So far, the noon meals had been rather grim occasions.

One of the tablemates was extremely quiet, rarely saying anything beyond a brief greeting. The second woman was a complaining type, offering negative comments about either the food, the temperature of the room, or some perceived carelessness on the part of the staff—something. The third woman, like so many of her fellow residents in the nursing home, seemed indifferent to everything; lost in a narrow world of her past.

I guess you might say our table is not the most congenial in the dining room, observed the old woman. As she neared the table, she was relieved to see she was the first to arrive. She would have time to consider a remedy for the dullness of the noon meal.

"I think there is something of August in all of us!" she said as she rolled her chair up to the table. "We seem to breathe hot and cold, poised on the verge of something different for which we are not too well prepared."

She knew the summer season took a great toll on old people. Keeping pace through the heated summer sapped their spirit. Even in a nursing home, some old people felt exhausted by perceived demands. A woman could become exhausted just thinking of all the things she imagined others expected her to do. She remembered her own maternal grandmother complaining through August at the unwonted heat, even as she maintained a working pace that staggered younger women. Could that explain some of the difficulty she felt in her tablemates?

"Hello there," the old woman said as the first tablemate appeared and sat in the chair on her left. She was determined to get a conversation started with a pleasant greeting.

To her surprise, the tablemate looked up and smiled warmly at her.

"Are you having a good day?" the tablemate asked. This was a safe, standardized question to ask of anyone in the nursing home, although it could initiate a flood of complaints about different aches and pains. No complaints were expressed, however, and the two women continued to exchange pleasantries for a minute or so before the third woman in the group joined them.

Her arrival coincided with that of the food trays. The old woman in the wheelchair nodded pleasantly at her and pointed to the food being served. “I really like it when they serve this menu. The vegetables are cooked perfectly, and the chicken is baked to perfection.” She hoped her voice sounded friendly, and she was careful to say everything with a smile.

To her surprise, the woman across from her looked up, squinting as if to see for certain who was talking. She took a bite of the chicken, then one of carrots.

“Yes, it’s good food,” the woman across from her answered. “I like the meals, all of them. Some days I am simply not hungry because I don’t feel so good. Hard to get excited about any meal if your stomach is in revolt.”

She must be feeling good today, the old woman observed, *for she seems intent on eating every bite.*

By now the fourth woman had arrived, just in time to catch the last bit of conversation. After apologizing for her tardiness, she offered her own comment on the meal: “The best part of the meal is dessert! I always enjoy the dessert.”

She examined the slice of chocolate cake that went with the meal and added, “I’ve had a sweet tooth all my life, and dentures didn’t change it a bit!” The other three laughed with her at her little joke.

The four women continued to make small talk during the remainder of their meal and even lingered at the table after the trays were removed. The old woman in the wheelchair was the first to leave, bidding them all a pleasant afternoon.

"Glory be," she remarked under her breath as she wheeled herself away. "They have all made my earlier impressions of them completely invalid. What on earth is so different about this rather tired and weary day in late August? By all my earlier accounts, they should be tired and grouchy, the way they seemed to be yesterday."

She had become much better acquainted with the women during this lunch. Until today, she only knew their names. Today, however, they happily talked among themselves, sharing interesting information about themselves.

The old woman had not gone very far from the table when she heard one of the women, who was a trifle deaf, say loudly to the other two, "Wonder what got into her today? She was different—friendly and pleasant."

The old woman was shocked out of complacency. Without her, it seemed the other three had little trouble being pleasant to one another. Could it possibly be that it was *she* who communicated poorly, who was inclined to complain? Was she withdrawn and unwilling to share with her tablemates?

In her room, she thought about that wonderful poem by Robert Burns, "To a Louse." The poet described a conceited young girl sitting in front of him at church. Anyone could tell the girl thought herself better than anyone else by the way she tossed her head. She wore a beribboned bonnet, and the poet watched the girl surreptitiously scratching about her hairline and the ribbons of the bonnet. Then he noticed the presence of a louse burrowing about! The girl was carefully trying to keep anyone from spotting the creature's presence as her finger gently sought to get rid of it. How awful if anyone should discover that she, a woman of impeccable social class, had a head full of lice!

Too late, however, because the immortal Scottish poet recorded for all generations ever after to enjoy:

O wad some gift the giftee gie us,
To see oursels as ithers see us!

The old woman remembered that when explaining the poem to her children and grandchildren, she had to translate the Scottish dialect into this: "Oh, would some gift the Giver give us, that we could see ourselves as others see us!"

"Ah, mercy," the old woman sighed. "I may have seemed an older version of that young woman, so possessed with airs about her importance! Where have I been all this time since being admitted to this rest home?"

"I have been too lost in my own thoughts," she said; "absorbed with my own aches and pains. I wanted to blame the heat of August when it was my indifference to those around me that made me—and them!— uncomfortable."

After she settled herself down for her afternoon nap, she made a promise to herself. "Life at every stage demands that we give something good of ourselves to others. My silence has kept me occupied pleasantly with the past, but it is the present that I am living, and I need to make a contribution to it."

"This is my wake-up call," the old woman said as she contradicted herself and settled into her afternoon nap.

September

After the hot flush of summer subsides,
September arrives to offer new beginnings,
fresh challenges.

A Song for September

The old woman in the wheelchair made her way down the corridor of the wing where her room could be reached near the end. The soft, filtered light of a mid-September sun cast dancing patterns on the shiny tile floor, giving her a feeling of joy and putting a song in her heart. She had been here now for several years and had long ago made a good adjustment to life in the nursing home.

At first she missed terribly all the freedom of movement and choice that had described her life on the small farm near the edge of town, but the security and safety of being looked after gave her great comfort. Her children and grandchildren visited her often, and she remained a very important figure in their lives.

What did people do in those years before assisted living and nursing facilities were available for the aged and infirm? She thought back in her own life to recall what had become of her grandparents and aunts and uncles. With a shock, she realized that none of them had actually lived to a very great age.

It was not uncommon in those days for people to head toward eternity while in their early sixties. Now, thanks to the advances of medicine, more and more of the older generation were living well past eighty and ninety years of age. Some, like herself, were unable to live safely at home because serious physical problems kept them bound to a wheelchair. With a little rueful laugh, she said to herself that she would be glad when the advance of medicine made it possible for old folks to stay on their feet!

Once upon a time she had been very steady on her feet. She remembered being a more than capable athlete, and when teams were chosen in the schoolyard games, she was always among the first selected, and with good reason, too. She could catch any ball thrown in her direction, and at bat, she would always hit the ball, usually to the outfield, where the less talented players lolled around, incapable even of catching cold.

One September afternoon when school was out, she was playing a game of softball on the side lawn of the farm. The other players were her sisters and a number of cousins. They had improvised to create the bases: several bricks placed to form a square marked first, second, third, and home. She put all her reputation for competitive toughness on the line, even in this game of small consequence. She hit a ball to the outfield and knew she could reach third—but could she stretch it and make it all the way home? She raced toward the last square of bricks, but could see that a strong-armed cousin had chased down the ball and thrown it to home. She knew she would have to slide, and slide she did, right across the bricks, her right hand extended.

Amid the cheers of her team, she checked herself over to see what all had been hurt. First, to her chagrin, she had broken three fingernails on her right hand. Not to worry, though, they would grow back. The pain on her narrow right hip bone, however, was something else. She saw blood appearing on the right side of her slacks and knew the skin had been broken. That, too, would grow back, she consoled herself as she limped to the little garden bench that had been hauled into service for the game.

She was right. The fingernails were flourishing and lovely within a few weeks, and the torn skin on her bony hip healed even faster. But beneath that skin, the bone itself remained unhappy the rest of her life. Through the years, she had trouble with the entire right side of her body. *Peculiar,* she thought. *It was my hip bone, not my ear!* Yet she had earaches every winter thereafter in the right ear. When she had a bad throat infection, the pain and soreness moved down her body and settled in the right side! Later in life, it was her right hip that broke so badly it caused her to be placed in the wheelchair. She thought she must surely have a very weird body.

As she considered her physical infirmities, she wondered if they must be part of some eternal message worth examining. She thought of that old saying, "a chain is only as strong as its weakest link." Weak links applied to more than chains and bodies. She remembered the flood tides that threatened the farm during hurricane seasons. The water sought the weakest fortifications; therefore her father had paid special attention to those spots he perceived were weak.

It took only a moment to come up with another example. A teacher who loves the class assigned to her must identify those students who are weak. They are the ones who will need extra help in order to succeed. The old woman thought it must be that way with people throughout their lives: those fortunate enough to be strong must look after the weak.

She could remember her beloved grandmother, who had given so much to her when she was a small child in need of extra attention. She was not yet four, and her mother was preoccupied with two babies younger than herself. It was her grandmother who took her under her wing and gave her the maternal attention she needed. When this grandmother became very ill near the end of her life, she could remember going to her house to help out.

One of the tasks she did for her grandmother was to iron the clothes. Although she was only twelve or so at the time, she heated the "sad iron" on the stove and set to work on the clothes basket of ironing. She even tried to iron her granddaddy's khaki pants. A neighbor had dropped in to see how things were getting along and commented favorably on her enterprise.

Her granddaddy came into the room and bragged about her to the neighbor, saying, "She has ironed those khaki pants so slick that a fly slides right off them." This was all the praise she needed to continue a task that most housewives have always hated to do.

She remembered that her grandmother was ill for several years before she passed away, and except for two hospital stays, she remained at home. The family took turns caring for her, and it was done in a spirit of joy and thanksgiving. This grandmother was a giant among them, and she would be sorely missed. She may have been a tower of strength and generosity, but illness brought about a role-reversal for all of them.

For her, helping a beloved grandmother had provided her with life lessons that would continue to serve her well as she grew into maturity. Ever after, she took special pains with weakness wherever it appeared. The weakness might be in a child, even her own, who temporarily was in need of a boost from a sensitive adult. The weakness might be in a neighbor or loved one whose illness was devastating. If she could give a helping hand, she willingly and generously gave one.

Sometimes, she acknowledged, the weakness was simply in herself. It was a good thing to examine herself periodically and take stock, mentally, physically, and spiritually. If any area was weak and needed attention, she prayed for the good sense to put things right.

Now that she thought about it, putting things right was that beloved grandmother's lifestyle. No wonder hardly a day passed that the heritage the grandmother had passed on to her was not acknowledged with gratitude. "I think I have patterned so much of my life after hers," the woman in the wheelchair said to herself, "that it helps me understand the overall success and happiness of my own life. It comes from living outside myself, as my grandmother did, and being responsive to the needs of others."

The old woman knew that the days of responding to the needs of others had largely passed, because her own infirmities had circumscribed her life to such a high degree. Then she caught the direction of this kind of thinking and did an about-face.

"Thank the Lord, my mind and spirit are A-one. Who said all help must be physical? Just as I am, I can still be of service to others."

She picked up a book of daily devotions and headed back up the hallway. A friend of hers, blind now for several years, depended on her to read to her daily. It was a service she looked forward to every day.

Sounds of music drifted from one of the nursing home's small living rooms. It was just the right cadence to match the progress of her wheelchair as she made her way toward the waiting welcome of her old friend.

Psalm to Age

Lord, thank You for giving me the years
To fill with friendships and love,
To absorb as much of the earth's beauty
As my senses could accommodate.

Lord, thank You for allowing me
To call upon You at will,
Because my uncertain steps
Often needed abrupt correction.

Lord, thank You for the inner peace
That enabled me to see beyond
The difficulties of the moment
And focus on the deeper lessons of life.

Lord, thank You for the wit and wisdom
Imparted to me by others;
They have been true Angels in my life,
And they pointed the way toward You.

Lord, thank You for the signs of age
My tired and wrinkled face betray;
They are testimony of the many years
You trusted me to live well.

The Silver Clarinet

The noisy day was almost over. It had been a happy noise, but the old lady in the wheelchair was tired and needed the sanctuary of her own room. A dozen students from a local junior high school band played a brief concert for the residents in the nursing home. To some, like the old woman in the wheelchair, the concert seemed much longer. She had enjoyed the program, but part of her desire to return to her room was that she was hearing the steady beat of music from her past.

It was a habit she had developed over the last decade of her life; using the present occasion to unite with something from her own earlier experience. "I suspect most of us old people do that," she had explained to her family. "Helps us to make sense of things if we can add something familiar to what is going on today."

She had been intrigued by the little clarinet player in the group, whose freckled face and slight form were so reminiscent of her own former self. Mostly, she had been fascinated by the silver clarinet the little girl played. She had once played such an instrument as a sixth grader oh-so-many years ago.

Shutting her eyes and sitting very still as she always did when summoning up the past, the old woman saw her school's new band teacher walk into her classroom to urge the youngsters to join the band. It would be a step they would benefit from all their lives, he promised. Many of the students responded to this invitation and learned the only thing standing between them and full band membership was the acquisition of a musical instrument. Instruments could be ordered from Chicago, and order blanks were distributed.

She was told that her size seemed a good fit for the clarinet, whatever that meant. Her larger classmates were encouraged to play saxophone or the trombone. She took the information on the clarinet home with her after school and told her parents, "I've got to get a clarinet."

Her startled parents, unaccustomed to this rather shy daughter ever making demands, began to explain that there was no money available for such an expense. The little sixth grader was insistent, and the parents agreed to fill out the order blank and mail it off to Chicago. They would pay for the clarinet in several installments.

For the next several weeks, the young girl raced to the post office every day after school to see if her clarinet had arrived. The postmistress, annoyed at first by this earnest little girl, eventually recognized the importance of the anticipated package.

In the meantime, the girl sat in band class in the clarinet section, learning the music and playing an imaginary clarinet. She soon knew the location of all the keys and the fingering necessary to play the note shown on the sheet of music. Some of the others already had their instruments, borrowed from an older brother or sister, but others, like herself, played imaginary instruments as they learned to read music.

During band class, as the little girl faithfully played her imaginary instrument, she heard the music in her head and knew she was part of the band. Everything the music teacher had explained was true: being a band member was very special. Everyone in the band was a friend to everyone else. She was beginning to learn the meaning of *esprit de corps*, and it added a rich dimension to her life.

Eventually—it had only been a few weeks, but seemed forever to the little girl—the postmistress smiled at her as she walked through the door. The little girl detected from the smile that this was the day, and she could hardly keep from hopping about as the postmistress handed her the long, skinny box that had arrived from Chicago. The little girl raced all the way home, a considerable distance, and opened the box in the presence of her family.

Was ever an instrument greater loved than that little silver clarinet? The little girl could not imagine such a thing. She saw the clarinet as a symbol of friendship, for it had been her passkey to band membership. In the band, she had found it easy to break from her essential shyness and make friends. The camaraderie developed among those students endured years beyond school. *Esprit de corps* forever! It was a perpetual Sousa march playing in her mind.

As adults, she and her closest friends attended a stage show of the popular musical, *The Music Man.* They, more than most in the audience, understood the play's deeper message. They had also been brought together by their own "music man" as little sixth graders. They, too, had played upon imaginary instruments to learn the notes and fingering before they actually held a real instrument in their hands. They were quick to pay tribute to their own music man, and to those music men in the lives of students in schools everywhere.

The old woman recalled that the little silver clarinet had been her instrument in the band for three years. Then she became a member of the high school band, and alas, she would have to play the more sophisticated black wooden clarinet. She laid the little silver clarinet aside, but never forgot its importance. She knew it symbolized something greater than the sum of its shiny keys. It was kept in a closet with other school mementos, and through the years, she would occasionally take it out and play simple tunes on it.

By now she was married and had children who were fascinated with the little instrument. They recognized its importance to their mother, because it was safely stored in the closet many years after the key pads had dried up and fallen off, and its shiny form had tarnished as neglected silver will.

By this time the children were grown and no longer living at home. Christmas was approaching, and collectively, they wondered what they could possibly give their mother that she would appreciate. They came up with the perfect idea, and Christmas morning, a gift under the tree was unmistakably the size and shape of a clarinet case. The mother was astonished to see that it was indeed her own silver clarinet, shiny bright again and restored to playing condition.

She played little tunes for her family, and as she did she became the little sixth grader of her childhood. She was surrounded again by a band of friends keeping beat to the music directed by their music man. He had been right. The magic of the silver clarinet had endured.

The power of the little clarinet didn't stop with the impromptu concert she gave her children. Years passed, and the woman and her friends were celebrating the fiftieth anniversary of their graduation from high school. The woman was in charge of the reunion, and she planned displays in the great hall where the classmates would be congregating.

There were tables with letter jackets and trophies on them, and tables with diplomas and other framed documents. The table that seemed to attract the greatest attention, however, was the one that celebrated the band. It had pictures, programs, sheet music, and a band uniform. In the center, commanding most attention, however, the little silver clarinet stood proudly next to a dented but shiny brass trumpet. They were relics from that sixth-grade class of students who dared to understand the invitation of the music man, and to learn the power of *esprit de corps.*

That reunion was a tremendous success, the old woman recalled, as were all the reunions with her friends through the years. Because all of them had been band members, many of their shared experiences were band-related. Their music man had told them membership in the band would be valuable all their lives, and he had been right; right in ways no sixth grader could ever have imagined.

"You just had to listen to the music," the old woman mused to herself. It was a siren call of considerable charm and strength.

As she made herself ready for bed, her thoughts returned to the little sixth-grade girl with freckles who had been part of today's concert for the nursing home's residents.

"I hope she plays that little silver clarinet with all her heart and soul. It will repay her all the years of her life."

October

What's to love about October?
Everything!
It's the autumn's perfect
Complement to Spring.

Fog

What had become of the sun? Yesterday had been bright and full of sunshine, but today, fog enveloped everything. The old woman in the wheelchair was always unsettled by fog. When fog obscured the surroundings she knew very well, she felt she had been displaced into some unknown dimension.

Although she wore glasses and could not read without them, she was very proud of her vision. Most people of her advanced age were unable to see very much, and glasses did not help their vision to any great extent. *It must be as if they are in a constant fog*, the old woman thought, shuddering.

What a terrible fate it must be to awaken every morning to a fog: "lost in a fog" had a deeper, sadder meaning.

The old woman considered the five senses and was grateful that she still possessed sufficient strength in all of them. Many years ago, she engaged in a conversation with a close friend, who was a musician, about the relative merits of sight and sound. To her surprise, her friend said she would prefer to be deaf than blind.

"But never to hear music again? How awful that would be," she said to her friend.

There was much more than music in her friend's life, however. There were the great art museums the two of them visited and the splendid scenery along the way of the trips they made together. There were the faces of their children, and hopefully, there would be the faces of grandchildren and great-grandchildren in the years to come.

For herself, there was additionally an overwhelming love of color. She was always puzzled when asked to name her favorite color. It was almost as ridiculous a question as to name her favorite child. She honestly loved all colors, and she thought it was magnanimous of God to create a world so rich in the various colors of nature. Furthermore, nature waxed and waned in its tints and hues, providing the seasons with a continual change of artistic whimsy. Who wouldn't choose vision over any other sense, simply to enjoy nature's palette?

When she was a small child, she favored yellow. She well remembered being made to stand in the corner in her first grade classroom because she had disobeyed the teacher's instruction. The children were given a sheet to color, with suggestions of the appropriate crayons to use: the suit the man in the picture wore should be brown, black, or dark blue. The car he was about to get into could be green, black, or maybe white. Her little six-year-old self thought these colors would produce a dreary picture, so she picked up her yellow crayon and splashed it all over the page. Yellow car, yellow suit on the man, yellow, yellow, everywhere yellow.

She was satisfied; her teacher was irritated at yet another indication of rebellion in the little girl. The corner wasn't so bad, she told herself. She could face the blank wall and lose herself in her thoughts, which were far more interesting than figuring out how to make a brown suit and a green car into an interesting coloring exercise. Perhaps this early school experience became the starting point in her life for all the introverted thinking that had become her habit.

Yellow remained her favorite color for many years, but eventually she decided that a pure sky blue was equally beautiful. It was the color of heaven. After that, favorite colors came and went with her altering moods, until that happy day of maturity when she decided she liked color; all of it and lots of it.

To be deprived of color in her life would be tragic for her. She considered the fog, which temporarily made everything a soft gray. There was great danger in that softness. It obscured all the shapes and locations of what should be familiar.

The old woman recalled a poem written by Carl Sandburg:

The fog comes
On little cat feet.
It sits looking
Over harbor and city
On silent haunches
And then moves on.

The fog in the poem was not a house cat, waiting quietly for its dish to be filled, but a large and powerful jungle cat, poised to strike its prey, the harbor and city. And then, as mercurial as weather itself, the fog cat changes purpose and lifts itself from the scene. The familiar shapes of the city emerge.

As the old woman looked out the window, she saw the fog cat begin to lift. For a moment or two she wanted it to remain, for she had yet another idea she wanted to pursue, and the fog was her point of inspiration.

Where had the thought gone? Wisps of it remained, as did faint strands of fog she could see beyond her window. She thought about the perpetual fog some of the residents in the home seemed to be living in. Perhaps they were as successful in their fog as she had been looking out at hers. As she saw the fog, she used the occasion to remember many things that had been important in her life. They were little snippets of memory that could be threaded together in a meaningful way.

She loved those snippets, and she never tired of rearranging them, much as an artist might decide to paint the trees in the picture a golden hue of autumn rather than a fresh green of early spring. She decided that those residents who seemed so lost to the present might actually be involved in their own collections of snippets to play with and arrange, choosing their own colors, without fear of contradiction.

For them, the fog cat was gentle and forgiving. Perhaps its favorite color was yellow.

To My Old Friend

Do you recall the carefree days when
We were young?

How we explored the limits of our world,
Carefully keeping within the bounds
Of grace and propriety?

Through books we learned about
A vast, exciting world beyond our town,
Unlimited by time or place.

We indulged our appetite to explore these books
And failed to comprehend
Why too often the exploration

Was a journey made by us alone,
Our other friends disdaining
Our singular appreciation of the past.

Art, history, music, and all the
Epochal makers of human achievement
Inspired and excited our growing imagination.

Now we are no longer young,
And physical limitations are drawn tighter.

The books are still there, and
The study of a lifetime makes me find
Them more exciting and inspiring than ever.

When I reach for a familiar volume,
Or discover a new one that illuminates,
I am reminded of those habits of our youth.

It is then I want to preach to my grandchildren
And their friends:

Turn off the TV
Lay down the Cell Phone
Pick up a book and Read!

Penny for Your Thoughts

The old woman in the wheelchair was outside in the crisp sunshine of a beautiful day in October. It was a pleasure to enjoy a beautiful day like this in late October. She well knew that autumn would be the prelude to winter, and when the weather turned cold, her bones would complain. *Enjoy this beautiful day*, she said to herself, *who knows when such a one will come again for you!*

As she pushed her wheelchair along, she spotted a dull, copper penny on the sidewalk in front of her, just at the edge of a flowerbed where workmen had recently been digging. *I must find some way to pick it up*, she said, *because a penny is a lucky thing to find.* She laughed to think of this mild superstition, but it was one she'd held all her life. It would be interesting if she could know how many copper pennies she had picked up and the places they had been found. There had been many years; too many places; far too many pennies for her even to guess.

At that moment, one of the nurses approached her, and the old woman said, "Would you do me a favor and pick up that lucky penny I have found?"

The nurse laughed and bent down to pick up the penny. As she handed it to the old woman she said, "I have little superstitions myself … I guess one of yours is to pick up a penny when you find one."

The old woman smiled in embarrassment and explained, "I know a penny isn't worth much, but it always gives me pleasure to pick one up. I think it was my grandmother many years ago who said to pass up one of these small coins was to miss a possible blessing. So I always pick them up."

She thanked the nurse after receiving the coin and placed it in the little pocket device on her wheelchair where she kept a packet of tissues, a pad of paper, and a good writing pen.

Why did the nurse call it a superstition? the old woman asked herself. *I never thought of it as a real superstition, but more like an acknowledgement that many small things in life are blessings, and we must be thankful for all of them. Am I a superstitious person?*

"A penny for my thoughts!" she said aloud in a laughing voice. "A penny can't really bring luck … and even if it did, what is luck?"

Her thoughts now took a different turn. The old woman didn't think she had ever really believed in luck, but more in personal effort and hard work. She had always done well in school, but there was no luck attached to it. What she had done to achieve her success was to behave well in class, follow the teacher's instructions, do her homework, and prepare for tests. That wasn't luck! That was a formula. Some little thought at the back of her mind demanded to be heard: what about that kid who always did well on true/false tests and multiple-choice questions? True, she remembered such a boy in elementary school who had phenomenal success with such tests.

Try as she might, she could not remember his name. He was not a very good student, because he never really cared for school. However, he could ace the objective tests! It turned out that he was quite good at eliminating the fairly obvious wrong answer and the probably wrong answer of four choices. That left him only two to choose from, and he was, more often than not, able to choose the correct one. The odds were fifty/fifty! On the true/false questions, he could spot the one word that made a statement false. But this was not an exhibition of subject knowledge—the old woman never agreed with her classmates that "he was just lucky." She knew he wasn't lucky; merely good at spotting errors and making choices.

Ultimately, he made a number of wrong choices. She recalled that he became a big gambler, and when some early successes went to his head, he then plunged in *over* his head and wound up in prison. Luck? *I think not,* she said, *More like just desserts!*

When her own very happy, successful marriage was being talked about among her friends, some of those whose marriages had been miserable would say, "She was so lucky!"

Luck had nothing to do with it, the old woman said in reflection of her more than sixty years of happy marriage. It had all to do with *love, consideration,* and *kindness.*

She well recalled one morning when she and her husband were talking about the elements of a happy marriage. They both agreed that one had to start with love. Looking into his handsome face and seeing the familiar gentle features, she said she thought consideration was another important element.

Always he had been considerate of her needs, often forgoing his own plans to participate in something that was important to her. He added that kindness was just about as important as love, for without it, the love wouldn't last. She had agreed, thinking as she did that no one could have been more kind than this wonderful man she had married. So much for luck in producing a happy marriage!

They had successfully raised four lovely children, a son and three daughters. All of them had turned out well, had married well, and had raised their own children with great success. Where was the luck in all of this success? To chalk it up to luck was to ignore all the serious hard work the parents had devoted to the raising of their children.

She reached into the pocket where the penny was and removed it to rub off some of the encrusted soil. With shock, she realized that it was not an ordinary penny with Abraham Lincoln's chiseled features on it, but a rare Indianhead penny, worth a considerable amount of money.

"Well now," the old woman considered as she rubbed the penny between her fingers. "Perhaps there is a kind of luck in life after all. How did I come to possess this penny of great value at just this time of my life?" She remembered the nurse who had kindly picked it up for her. This was the same nurse, she recalled, who was having a great deal of trouble in her life because of a family illness.

"I still don't think it's luck," said the old woman, "but *providence.* It is a reminder that the Lord provides.

"My part in this little episode is to find the nurse and tell her about the penny, its value, and that it now belongs to her. It has been my blessing, not my luck, to be a participant in this little story about a lucky penny."

November

This month is favored for reflection,
For taking note of the cornucopia
Of blessings we enjoy, and
Celebrating Thanksgiving.

Remembering the Day

The old woman wheeled herself up to the small desk tucked away in the library. This was where she liked to take care of her correspondence, and today she had a long list of loved ones on her mind.

She had asked for a box of Thanksgiving cards, and one of her granddaughters had brought one to her yesterday. She loved the design on the cards: a lovely cornucopia overflowing with all kinds of fruits and vegetables, surely one of the most favored of Thanksgiving symbols.

She liked the verse inside, too, which said, "May the bounty of God richly bless us, and may we in turn be a blessing to others. Have a happy Thanksgiving Day!" She hoped she had always been a blessing to others, and she knew that she had certainly been the recipient of a cornucopia of blessings spilled out generously in her direction all her life.

"I couldn't have said it better myself." The old woman smiled in reflection. "Hasn't God always been good to me? From the earliest Thanksgiving I can remember until this year and the one coming up next week."

I have never been hungry. There were years during the Great Depression when I hardly knew where my next meal would come from, but there always seemed enough to make a good Thanksgiving dinner for my family, and even enough to share with neighbors who had less than we did. Then, during the war years, some ingredients were unavailable, but we all learned to manage with what we had, and a Thanksgiving dinner materialized somehow and never disappointed. Perhaps just not as sweet. She laughed to herself, recalling the rationing of sugar.

I have never been without hope. Admittedly, there were tough times—that war, for instance, which took her husband off to the army for a while. "Yes, that was tough, but we made it through that difficulty, always believing that we would be together again," she said. Other tough times followed, but stronger than the difficulties were the love and trust that dominated her marriage.

I have never been without love. She remembered her treasured childhood, where she learned the meaning of love from devoted parents who created a home filled with careful nurturing of their children. She especially liked to recall the Thanksgiving when she was about ten years old. Those years were hard for her parents, because there wasn't much money to stretch in all the directions required for a growing family of five young children. She remembered her father had briefly taken a second job to relieve some of the economic stress. At no time, however, had her mother indicated that a Thanksgiving dinner with all the trimmings would be an impossibility that year.

To the contrary, she remembered this particular dinner as a highlight among all the special dinners of her life. Her parents had invited an aunt and uncle and their three children to join them, and this brought the number to be fed at the table to an imposing dozen! This particular family was having a rough time of it—her uncle having lost his job a couple of months ago. How would her mother manage?

Always hopeful in her belief that providence would bless their existence, her mother went about planning the dinner. Out in the hen yard, the centerpieces of that meal had been pigging out for several months, never questioning the extra rations of corn, but gobbling every kernel thrown their way. Yes, two fattened hens were going to grace the Thanksgiving table. Her mother knew how to stretch that beginning by creating a dressing of cornbread, celery, onions, sage—oh my, the memory of her mother's cornbread dressing always produced the most pleasant memories of delightful dining. These ingredients were not expensive, and her mother had always started setting aside what she would need in early September so that November never caught her without.

The fruits from various trees had been saved from the seasonal harvest and rested in glassy rows upon the pantry shelf. Several of those jars would be combined to create a perfect fruit salad. Her mother always added pecans, and these had been collected by the children just a few weeks ago. They had been shelled in the evenings as the children sat around the fireplace, listening to their parents read from the Bible.

Also in glass jars on that pantry shelf were green beans and other vegetables, a testimony to the generous garden that had fed them well all summer. In the barn, a special crib held buckets of potatoes. Her mother knew how to cook them to perfect tenderness, so that when mashed, they produced mounds of delightful pleasure. Every child in the family loved the mashed potatoes and gravy only their mother knew how to make perfectly every time.

There was one thing that absolutely necessitated an expense beyond the providence of good kitchen planning, but this year there was simply no money to be had for the cranberries. No visit to the local grocer was planned; they would have to do without. The cranberries were grown somewhere else and were relatively expensive, so they would not be bought for the dinner this year. Nor would there be celery in the dressing; that was the one vegetable the garden simply refused to produce for the table. Her mother had laid aside the necessary syrup to use in baking the pecan pies. How many mornings had the children complained that their pancakes didn't have enough syrup on them? Firmly their mother insisted that the syrup had to be rationed this month, and they ceased complaining, knowing even at that early age they could trust their mother's judgment.

When the aunt and uncle and cousins arrived that Thursday morning of Thanksgiving, their very arrival announced a holiday atmosphere. Further, each member of that family walked through the door carrying their own contribution to the meal.

The aunt had baked a wonderful cake—she was the best cake baker in the family, and the uncle was carrying a tray of homemade rolls ready to be placed in the oven. One cousin was carrying small bags of homemade candy for everyone, another was carrying a beautiful bowl of whipped butter. The oldest cousin proudly held up her mother's finest cut-glass bowl filled with cranberry sauce. "I knew you would need it," the aunt said. She explained that the uncle had secured a job a week ago, and his first paycheck allowed them to indulge in this generous display of sharing.

What a party they enjoyed, all in the middle of a big, economically bad time for everyone. The old woman, in reflection, thought it must have seemed like some of the heartwarming scenes from Charles Dickens's *A Christmas Carol*, only she knew that every bit of it was just as she remembered it.

Yes, the food was delicious, and everyone had all they could eat, with leftovers for a meal yet to come. The thing about that dinner, so well remembered all these years, was its spirit of peace and goodwill. It was a day full of many good things, but the greatest blessing of all was the bounty of love that united them.

As the old woman began to address the Thanksgiving cards, the first three were to those well-loved cousins who had been her dear friends all these years. And in her heart, she felt a surge of thankfulness to their parents and to her own dear mother and father, who knew how to create an environment of love and security for their families. They had served as virtual cornucopias all year long and every year, endlessly producing love and comfort for their children.

What a precious heritage God has blessed me with! The old woman was wreathed in smiles as she addressed all the envelopes and placed stamps on them.

Next week, when her granddaughter took her to celebrate Thanksgiving with her family, she must remember to share with them the story of how, with so little, so much was produced to make two families completely happy.

Granddaddy's Holiday

Every kid in our family knew it at an early age.
Granddaddy preferred Thanksgiving.
Preferred it to the Fourth—
Too hot to celebrate a holiday.
Preferred it even to Christmas—
Too much bustling about,
Too many expensive gifts to buy.
Might leave someone out.

We suspected that this rather
Portly Granddaddy had another
More tasteful reason for
Preferring Thanksgiving.
Grandmother took great pains
To stimulate appetites
By aromas drifting from the kitchen
Into all recesses of the house.
When we knew we couldn't wait
A single moment longer,
She called, "Let's gather for dinner!"

She was a fantastic cook, and her
Culinary reputation was secure,
Based on several delightful dishes,
Which she served every Thanksgiving.
No one appreciated her gift
More than Granddaddy.
Long after we kids had been
Excused from the table,
Granddaddy sat, comfortably full,
Dropping small morsels to
The little rat terrier who
Sat at his feet.

Yes, Granddaddy loved Thanksgiving,
But it took years of maturity
Before some of us recalled that
More often than not, he was a
True child of November, and
Thanksgiving was his birthday.

The Widow's Mite

When the old woman in the wheelchair had become a resident at the nursing home, she'd rebelled as her family knew she would. None of them wanted her to live there, but their choice was necessitated by concern for her ultimate well-being and safety. Her physical condition made living at home dangerous. No one in the extended family was free to look after her, for all were gainfully employed outside their homes. The nursing home provided the security and care they wanted for their mother.

It took a few months, but eventually the old woman made a good adjustment to the nursing facility. For one thing, whenever one of her great episodes of pain occurred, there was a nurse available to provide the necessary medication. She enjoyed interacting with the other residents, many of whom she had known all her life. She found the interaction challenging in many cases, because some of her old friends had deteriorated mentally. Had she been given a choice in the matter, she would choose her physical disabilities over the loss of mental competence. Each day she gave thanks for the blessing of a clear mind.

The old woman had always been an active participant in the outreach programs of her church and community. Helping her neighbors in whatever way she could was the practice of a lifetime. One of the reservations she had about becoming a resident at the nursing home was the loss of participation in what she termed her "good deeds for others." Although she could still respond with donations to the causes she supported, she missed the personal touch of helping individuals.

It was almost a year after she had entered the nursing home before she found she could still help her neighbors. Her children and grandchildren were very generous with gifts they thought appropriate for her, and she had a stockpile of perfumed lotions and other toiletries. These she used daily, but the stockpile grew. One morning, as she held her hand up to her face to catch the aromatic smell of fresh garden flowers, it occurred to her that she should share that hand cream with one of her friends.

For some weeks, she had been in the habit of visiting an old friend, now blind, and reading the Bible to her. Today she took along the tube of perfumed hand cream. She held her friend's hands in hers, then applied some of the cream, carefully rubbing it in.

"Now smell," she told her friend. "It's like a flower garden, isn't it?"

The smile on her friend's face was radiant. It was all the inspiration the old woman needed to make this a daily ritual as the Bible reading had become. She kept the tube of perfumed hand cream with her at all times, and she found other residents who enjoyed the application of scented flowers and the touch of a friendly hand. She became known as "the hand cream lady," and it was a label she cherished.

For years she had known that smell was the strongest of the senses, and that it stayed with the frailest of patients long after every other sense had failed. As her applications of hand cream continued, she knew this must be true, for even the most lethargic of her fellow residents responded to the aromatic scent of their hands after she had massaged the cream onto them.

This small outreach on her part did much to complete the adjustment of the old woman to her place in the nursing home. It was not an isolated activity, however, for the old woman spent time wondering what else she could do to be of service.

Her physical disabilities were greater than those most of her fellow residents endured, but she had all her senses intact. Sometimes she ruefully admitted she could do less with the sense of touch—wasn't that why she felt so much pain? Then she realized how foolish the thought was. It was the sense of touch, as much or more than the others, that protected a person.

One day in late November she was looking at her boxes of greeting cards to see how many Christmas cards she had on hand. Far too many, she noted. "The children must think I send out hundreds each year!" Like hand cream and lotions, they also brought her boxes of cards from time to time. She picked up a box and took it along with her to her blind friend's room.

"Let's address some holiday cards after we read the Bible," she said to her friend. The other old woman was taken aback, and she said she didn't have any cards. As with the hand cream, the cards were supplied, and in thirty minutes, several cards were addressed to the children and neighbors of the blind woman. "I'll just take these along with me and mail them with mine. I have plenty of stamps."

As she left her friend's room, the old woman wondered how many others in the nursing home might like to send a card or two, if only someone would supply the card and address the envelope. She went on a mission that day with two boxes of her cards, and by dinnertime that evening, she had been of assistance to at least a dozen fellow residents. She resolved that the next day she would complete the project and use the last of the cards in the second box.

Before she retired for the night, she telephoned her granddaughter and asked her to bring along a roll of stamps. "I know that postage has gone up, but I have the check ready to pay for a roll of one hundred."

If her granddaughter wondered why the old woman would be needing a whole roll of stamps, she was too polite to ask, and on her lunch hour the next day, she hurried into the rest home with the stamps. She found her grandmother at lunch, so she pulled up an extra chair and visited with the three women who shared the table with her. These old women thought how much the granddaughter and her grandmother resembled one another. Had they only known!

As the granddaughter moved her grandmother back to her room, she discovered the reason for the request for extra stamps.

"Why, Grand! What a marvelous thing to do. But this is a large facility, and I think you will need some help. Tomorrow is Saturday. I will bring some of the kids along with me, and we will help you with your project."

So it was that the holiday season saw as many cards going from the nursing home as the postman delivered to it. The cards could be counted, but how could the happiness be measured? The old people, cut off so many years from their active lives of special holiday traditions, rediscovered a joy in the season.

"And all because I discovered I had too many boxes of cards!" the old woman in the wheelchair exclaimed.

Preparations for the holiday season did not end, however, with the addressing and mailing of cards. The old woman called another granddaughter who was a buyer for a large department store to use her connections to supply a request.

"I know it's an imposition, but surely there are just boxes and boxes of those little perfumed lotion samples, and I would like to have as many as you can get for my friends at the nursing home."

This granddaughter was able to get small sample tubes of sufficient quantity to give to everyone at the home. The scents were varied, and there was a stir of activity as the old women compared the lilac scent with the rose, trying to determine which was lovelier.

Another granddaughter was able to get small packets of assorted greeting cards at a discount. Some stores she contacted were glad to donate complete boxes of them that had been around for a while. Before long, she had enough for everyone to have a packet of cards. She knew her grandmother would be helpful in seeing that the cards were used appropriately.

In less than a month, the old woman's inspiration to share had been multiplied into an air of happiness and satisfaction.

"Of course, I am the one who is the most satisfied and who is the happiest," she said to her visiting granddaughters. "It has given direction and purpose to my life. Perhaps I should say *re*direction of purpose, for I found myself again!

"It all started with a bit of perfumed hand cream—a kind of widow's mite—but look how powerful a mite can be!"

December

Christmas is in the Air—Everywhere!
People Meeting, Holiday Greetings,
The Hope of Promise Fair.

The Christmas Stocking

The old woman in the wheelchair stared at the Christmas stocking that had been given to her. Everyone in the nursing home had been given a similar stocking, and she knew it represented many hours of work and care and love on the part of those who gave out the stockings on Christmas Eve.

As she fingered the beautiful Christmas fabric of her stocking, she quietly wondered how many of her fellow residents in the home felt as she did about this gift of love; perhaps far more than anyone would have guessed. The outward reaction to the gift may, in some cases, have seemed unresponsive, but she knew that within each elderly person there was a soul touched by this display of love. And for many, like herself, the gift would send her thoughts in search of favorite Christmas memories.

The old woman gently moved her hand into the stocking and felt the pleasant shape of an orange. Didn't she have an orange in that very first Christmas stocking in her girlhood all those many years ago?

Yes, it was many, many years ago. She remembered well the Christmas when she was five years old. Times were hard; a war that involved the entire world had been completed, but a depression had replaced it and brought suffering closer to home. She remembered that there was very little extra to spend on Christmas. Her mother, God bless her, had five little girls talking about the coming of Christmas. How would she manage to provide them with a bright spot of happiness?

The woman smiled sweetly to herself as she remembered the sacrifice her mother had made for her little girls. There was one lovely dress her mother had worn for years, a treasured reminder of the days when she gaily danced her way through the seasonal holidays. It was cherry red and had silver lace trim around its neck, sleeves, and hem. She must have been a beautiful sight in this dress, dancing the Charleston with the man she would marry, and who would be the father of her five little girls.

The old woman, now deeply involved with this childhood memory, recalled clearly that her mother spent several evenings before Christmas in her bedroom, alone. At first the girls complained, but soon grew used to their mother's absence, and accepted their father's help with their homework and the household chores they were all assigned to do.

Imagine their surprise on Christmas morning to discover five beautiful red stockings hung on the fireplace, all vivid reminders of their mother's beautiful red dress! The stockings had that unmistakable trim—silver—around the top. The stockings bulged in enough places to let the girls know that they contained something. And what a something! The mother had used further fragments of her red dress to fashion clothing for little dolls she had made, using scraps of white, Indianhead cloth from her sewing basket. Each doll was different, and was each perfect for the little girl it was made for. The stocking also had a lovely orange in it, and pieces of handmade taffy. A shiny dime was discovered in the toe of each stocking.

Later generations may have thought this was not much of a Christmas, but the little five-year-old girl treasured its memory well into her own maturity. When she was a young mother herself, she was inspired by the red-stocking Christmas to guide her in providing her own children with similar memories. Their stockings were sure to contain something very special, too. The larger gifts under the tree could not compare in importance to the small gifts she managed to buy or make and place in the stockings. Always there was an orange. Always there was some kind of candy. And always there was the magic of adventure and exploration as the children examined the contents of the stockings.

She remembered that her youngest child, a boy, liked to hold his stocking close to him through the morning, exploring its contents slowly to make the joy of Christmas last. The older children, all girls, would rush to her and hug her in great bursts of joy. They had a good idea how much love and care had gone into the stockings and the small gifts inside. Their generation would carry on the tradition of the stocking.

When the children grew up, married, and had children of their own, she was privileged to see the tradition grow. Her daughters spent part of each pre-Christmas season making stockings for her grandchildren. Often she was able to participate, and one year, she embroidered each grandchild's name on the cuff of his or her stocking. From her own box of treasures she selected small trinkets of jewelry and wrote messages of love and hope for each grandchild. That was a very blessed Christmas, and she remembered it in great detail.

Where did all the Christmases go?

When the grandchildren were grown and having children of their own, she was not quite so involved. Still, she honored the family's stocking tradition, and with the help of one of her daughters, she went from store to store, finding just the right small gift to be placed in each great-grandchild's stocking. Her granddaughters were every bit as faithful about the stockings as her own daughters had been. *As she had been*, she reflected, and of course this acknowledgement took her back to the memories of her mother. Dear, devoted, and beautiful mother, who had not allowed the hardness of the age to destroy the magic and beauty of Christmas.

The beautiful red Christmas stocking in her early childhood had remained for her a symbol of what Christmas should be. And now, in the vintage years of her old age, she had a new stocking. Like her little son of so many years ago had done, she held it to her face and kissed it. She knew she would keep it close to her throughout the day as a reminder of the love of Christ shown through the love of others.

The old woman looked up at the others in the room, most of whom were looking as thoughtful as she imagined herself to be looking, and she whispered quietly to them all, "Merry Christmas."

Did she imagine it, or did she hear a chorus of angels singing, "Glory to God in the Highest, and on earth, Peace, Good Will to Men"?

So It Is

The autumn leaves have fallen
And most will disappear
Before we've passed December
And felt the coming year.

But after winter has its due
The trees' fresh leaves
Come bursting through.

(And in our lives, friends come and go;
Like autumn leaves, they come and go.)

The promise of the seasons is
The tree survives them all;

Trees bare in December
Will have leaves again next fall.

(Yes, the leaves will come again;
And so it is with friends.)

Joy for the Taking

The old woman in the wheelchair thought she might be a bit under the weather, so she decided to stay in her room and get some extra rest. The Christmas season was well underway, and she wanted to be strong enough to enjoy every special day of it. If she stayed in her room, she would not catch the germs of others or share her germs with them. Besides, she had some reading she had hoped to get to, and this would be the perfect time for that. Always at this time of the year, there were special television programs. Yes, a pleasant morning spent in her room would be just the thing to get her in good shape for the next two weeks of festivity.

She liked her room, and various members of her family came regularly to see that it was decorated for the season, and that all of her belongings were in proper order. The rest-home staff were very good about keeping it clean. *Come to think of it,* she thought, *this room and all those who make it so inviting are a great blessing to me. How fortunate I have been all my life to be surrounded by people who care about me.* The thought filled her with joy.

There was a remote control on her bedside table that turned on the television, and this year, there was another remote control that turned on the lights that decorated the small tree on top of the chest of drawers. She loved this little tree and its cheerful lights. Her great-granddaughter and great-grandson had been here last week with their mother, and they put it up for her, decorating it and showing her how the remote control could be used from her bed. What a convenience! Oh, the joy it gave her, the thoughtfulness of these great-grandchildren.

"Isn't it beautiful, Grand?" the girl had asked. The old woman's great-grandchildren called her *Grand*, because the oldest of them, a girl now almost thirty, had thought *Great-grandmother* too many syllables to handle. As a little child she had shortened the name to *Grand*, and this was the name used by all the little children who followed.

As the old woman settled into her comfortable chair and stared at the lights of the tree, she decided to leave the television off for a while and just relax with memories of past Christmas celebrations. She never tired thinking about these early years, when so many loved ones from the generation before her own were such a large part of her life. Her own beloved parents, grandparents, various aunts, uncles, and a number of cousins were the people who had enriched her life. If there was one good reason why she was grateful for her sound mind at her advanced age, it was because she could go back over the traces of her life, recalling the love and goodness provided by these loved ones.

The Christmas when she was barely six years old, for instance, was easy to recapture, partly because she played it over and over in her reminiscences and had all the details in perfect order. It was a difficult time, this period when she was so small, but a little six-year-old girl hardly knew it, because the adults in her life kept joy in their hearts. The joy expressed itself in smiles and hugs, in special little treats from the kitchen, and in excursions into the countryside. She well remembered when a favorite aunt drove up in her roadster. How proud her aunt was of this little car, and she wanted to drive her sister-in-law out in the country to show it off.

The old woman remembered her mother asking if they could possibly visit a wooded area and chop down a tree for Christmas. "Easy to do!" the jolly aunt announced. "We'll just plop it in the rumble-seat and have it home in no time at all."

There were several children about in the house, but this particular aunt had always favored her, and she invited her to go along on this special trip to secure a Christmas tree. The smaller children were left behind with their father.

When they reached a wooded area where many trees were growing, the aunt even allowed her to make the selection. Imagine that, a six-year-old getting to pick out the tree! This aunt knew instinctively how to make a little girl feel special and loved. To her childlike mind, no tree had ever been so aromatic, so green, so perfect for a family's Christmas. It took no effort even now for her to recall the rich pine smell of that tree. What a joy that entire tree excursion had been, and no wonder it held an honored place among her Christmas memories.

When she was nine years old, she discovered a new way to admire a Christmas tree: not from across the room, or even standing near it, but to lie down on the floor, with her head on the folds of the white sheet used to simulate snow around the tree, looking up into its branches. "This is a squirrel's eye-view of the tree," she said. She scanned all the ornaments hanging on the branches and realized that they all looked different from this vantage point.

I think I learned a lot from my upside down view of the tree, she reflected. *There are many ways to view any subject, just as every story has several sides.* Also, she remembered that the aroma of the tree seemed stronger when she was closer and looking up into its branches

She had never been preoccupied with the gifts beneath the tree, even in her youngest years. Always it was the tree itself that gave her the greatest joy in the days leading up to Christmas. Oh, she recalled with a bit of a shock, what about that Christmas when there was no tree?

This was a Christmas from her maturity—and her children were almost grown, too—when the whole family drove north to spend the holiday with loved ones they usually visited during the summer. Getting to spend Christmas with them in the winter had never happened, simply because of what they encountered on this trip. They had to ride behind a snowplow the last several miles to the farm. A terrible snowstorm had blanketed the entire state, and had it not been for the snowplow, who knows there they would have spent Christmas!

Her mother-in-law was almost in tears. "We have no Christmas tree. Until today we have been unable to get into town to get one, and now we have called in and they say they are sold out."

"We will manage," she remembered herself saying. She sent her husband out to the orchard to chop off a branch from an aging apple tree. Then she set her two girls to stringing cranberries. What seemed like miles and miles of cranberries and popped corn were strung together, then looped around the barren twigs and small branches of the larger branch. Her daughters looked through their grandmother's box of Christmas decorations and found many that could be used to fill out the blank spaces. *Now that was a tree to remember.* The old woman smiled at the memory.

The unique tree added grace and beauty to the Christmas scene, symbolizing that there was no problem the combined wits and efforts of the family couldn't solve. *Even at my mature age,* the old woman thought, *I was learning lessons. I think the greatest lesson of this unusual Christmas tree is that a person needs to be flexible. We may not be able to secure exactly what we had in mind, but ingenuity and flexibility will give us something that equally pleases and delights. It fills us with joy!*

"There is joy in the season, and it does not have to be wrapped in gold ribbon. As I look back in my reflections," the old woman considered, "it was never the gaily wrapped presents or fancy decorations; it was the presence of loved ones who filled my heart with joy. Even now, as an old woman with considerable aches and discomforts, life is full of joy because love is in my life."

Just as she concluded this thought, the phone rang, and it was another great-grandchild. "Hi, Grand." It was her oldest great-grandson, and he said he would be there in half an hour, and if she felt up to it, he would like to take her out for a drive to see the Christmas tree in the town square, whose lights had been turned on.

Was she "up to it"? Well, those germs and feelings of weariness she felt so protective about earlier simply vanished.

"I'll be ready, and can hardly wait to see you," she said to him.

Oh, the joy of love. It fills the air, and especially at Christmas. She said a little prayer of thanks.

THE END

LaVergne, TN USA
18 November 2009

164518LV00003B/1/P